WREN JANE BEACON ON THE CUT

BOOK FOUR

A NOVELLA BY

DJ Lindsay

See also:
Book One: 'Wren Jane Beacon Goes to War'
Book Two: 'Wren Jane Beacon at War'
Book Three 'Wren Jane Beacon Runs the Tideway'

www.wrenjaneb.co.uk

A CIP catalogue record for this book is available from the British Library.

Cover artwork from an original painting by Eric Bottomley GRA ©

Design: Alan Cooper, www.alancooperdesign.co.uk

Acknowledgements

My beta readers have been as eagle-eyed as ever (and they know who they are), but special mention must be made of Bev Walkling for her painstaking approach to the task.

Thanks are due to Michael Pearson for creating the map which made Jane's journey so much clearer.

Cath Turpin helped with commentary and advice on canal matters.

Staffs at the canal museums at Ellesmere Port, Stoke Bruerne, Gloucester and London were all helpful with my enquiries.

Jane Beacon retrospective

The Second World War was a major milestone on the road to equality for women. To survive Britain had to mobilise its entire population and with men called up into the forces women were drafted in to work in factories, to drive lorries and build bridges; to provide services for the uniformed forces without which they could not have functioned, and all this while keeping home and hearth going. By the war's end women were doing a myriad of things which had previously been thought beyond their abilities, and doing them very well. Never again could it be said that women were incapable, and this left a permanent marker for society.

This was achieved by each individual 'Doing their bit' and Jane Beacon was caught up in this maelstrom. Just nineteen when war was declared, her family's commitment to service saw her join the Women's Royal Naval Service (the 'Wrens') in October 1939. With a background in boats she was appointed the first experimental female crew hand on the Navy's harbour craft and made an outstanding success of it. Defying orders not to go, she took a cutter to Dunkirk and lifted over three thousand soldiers from the beaches. In its aftermath the Navy wanted to dismiss her for disobedience; the Army wanted to give her medals for her bravery.

The Army won that battle but she was marked in Naval circles as a troublemaker. Despite this her abilities could not be ignored and she was given a launch of her own to run with a Wren crew, operating on the River Thames during the Blitz. The success of this led to the Navy relenting its opposition to having Wrens crew its launches. At this time Jane Beacon helped a Lady Ormond survive the bombing of the Cafe de Paris in London. This led to the Lady, childless herself, informally adopting Jane and offering her the use of her extensive flat in Mayfair, as a London base. This proved a convenience which benefitted Jane throughout the war.

Jane Beacon might have been outstandingly successful as a boat cox'n. She was less so as a crew manager, hating the paperwork and administrative duties which came with the role. This led to a decision being made to deploy her instead on special projects, starting with being sent to Portsmouth to show the deeply doubtful authorities there that Wrens were quite capable of crewing boats. With a qualified success achieved there, her next special project was to take a trip on a narrow boat pair as the Wrens had been asked if they might provide crews for them.

In 1941 England's canal system was still a busy commercial network, moving freight between inland industrial areas and sea ports. The demands of war had greatly increased the traffic on them at a time when many of their male crew members were being called up into the forces and serious crew shortages were leading to badly needed canal boats being laid up. It was to offset this shortage that thought was being given to asking the Women's Royal Naval Service (Wrens) if they could crew the boats instead. The Wren authorities, suspecting that this was a very different world from running naval launches round its harbours, sent special projects Wren Jane Beacon to make a trip on a narrow boat pair and report on her conclusions. This book, the fourth in her saga, tells the story of that trip.

Dedication

To that most mis-named of groups, the Idle Women whose story prompted this tale.

Contents

WREN JANE BEACON
ON THE CUT

JANE'S JOURNEYS

Tamworth
Fazeley Junction
Polesworth
BIRMINGHAM 2
Atherstone
Bordesley Junction
Minworth
Nuneaton
Tyseley
Bedworth
Hawkesbury Junction
Knowle
Coventry
Rugby
Lapworth
Warwick
Braunston
D
Norton Junction
Hatton '21'
Leamington
Napton
Buckby
Northampton
Fenny Compton
Gayton Junction C
Stoke Bruerne
Cropredy
Wolverton
Banbury
Aynho
Bletchley
Heyford
Leighton Buzzard
Thrupp
Aylesbury
Marsworth
Tring Summit
Cowroast
Berkhamsted
Bablock Hythe
OXFORD
Hemel Hempstead
Lechlade
Watford
Kelmscott
Rickmansworth
Uxbridge
LONDON
Bulls Bridge
B A
Limehouse
Paddington Basin
Brentford
READING
Newbury

Jane's Journeys
Other Waterways
1 Grand Union Canal
2 Birmingham & Fazeley Canal ('The Bottom Road')
3 Coventry Canal
4 Oxford Canal
5 Upper Thames
A Islington Tunnel
B Maida Hill Tunnel
C Blisworth Tunnel
D Braunston Tunnel

CHAPTER ONE:
On Trial Again

Being sent to Portsmouth to show the authorities there how good a Wren – a woman – could be at boat handling was proving a difficult task. The launch was in difficulties as it tried to berth against the big seaweed-encrusted piles looming unforgivingly over it. The young killick cox'n threw his hands in the air in despair at the imminent disaster. "Catch a turn, catch a turn" he screamed; Petty Officer Wren Jane Beacon threw in two turns of the sternrope and hung on grimly. The boat bucked under full power as the cox'n struggled to stop it being swept down onto the pilings by the sluicing tide. She shrieked "Bloody idiot, turn her head to tide and you won't have this problem." The cox'n snarled and walked off the helm. "All right, if you're that clever, you do it." She thrust the rope tail into his hands, spun the wheel hard-a-port and stopped the port engine. Slowly, with only feet to spare, the boat turned and with its bow into the tide Jane had control of it. Juggling the two throttles she eased across the tidal stream and allowing it to turn the bow onto the berth as she got the boat alongside safely. "There, isn't that a bit better?"

The cox'n curled a lip silently at her.

An hour later she was summoned to the boats officer's office. "Beacon, it seems that you aren't really up to this. Chief Williams here tells me you didn't have a clue what to do this morning. He watched from the quay and was horrified by what he saw; the boat all over the place and you just waving your arms about."

"You what? I'm not having this, sir. It was that fucking idiot of a cox'n who got the boat into difficulties and abandoned the helm to me. It took me a minute to sort it out but I did and put her alongside properly."

"Beacon, do not swear at me. Chief Williams has been handling boats for longer than you've been alive and if he says you made a mess of it I believe him. I rather think the publicity which has preceded you was a bit misplaced."

"Sir, it is not misplaced. May I suggest that you let me run a boat for a week with Chief Williams on board to see for himself? That way I won't be getting judged by some other useless article's mistakes. You all seem more interested in proving me wrong than in seeing what I can do; all I ask is a fair crack of the whip."

"You've only got five days left here but I suppose we can put those to some sort of use. What do you think, chief?"

Chief Williams smiled grimly. "That would be long enough to find her out, sir. If you say so, I'll happily put this to the test."

"Right we'll put her into picket boat 127. You do know about picket boats, Beacon?"

"I've deckhanded on one but never had the controls. Steamers with a big slow-revving single propeller giving a huge kick to starboard going astern?"

"That's about right."

She had been warned that Portsmouth was less than friendly to the idea of Wrens in boats and had arrived ready to show them. After eighteen months working on Naval boats with some success she had no qualms about demonstrating her ability to handle them. The reality had been relegation to being stern hand and very little chance to show them any real ability to do more than throw a line. For two weeks her frustration had mounted but with clear orders to do as she was told and not to argue, all she could do was bite her tongue and try to look like an exceptional deckhand. Now was a chance to show them rather more.

Mustering in the boats officer's office five days later she felt rather better about the world. Her time in charge of picket boat 127 had gone well and although Chief Williams had cleared his throat rather noisily a couple of times he had said very little. Now a crucial moment was at hand. "Right, Chief, how did she do?"

"Well sir, better than I expected. Miss Beacon can certainly handle a boat and run a crew very effectively. She's a bit fond of coming in fast and relying on a hard kick astern to avoid banging into things which scared me a couple of times but she's certainly up to the job. It is difficult to fault her work but is she just one exceptional boat handler or does it suggest that women more generally can do this?"

The boats officer turned to Jane. "What do you say to that, young lady?"

"Training will be needed but why on earth should the fact that we are women make any difference to our ability to do the job? There's nothing about crewing launches which makes the job an intrinsically male one. Some level of physical fitness and strength is needed but believe me, there are plenty of women with that and where I can go, so can lots of other females. I don't think for a minute that you will find us any less competent or less hard working than the matelots you are used to."

On the train back up to London Jane reflected on the previous day's discussion. At the end there had been a sense of grudging acceptance, of another all-male redoubt lowering the drawbridge just enough to cross it. For the moment that was all she could ask for; with such entrenched prejudice it would clearly take more than five days for any full acceptance to follow. But at least she had managed a first marginal prising open of their minds. It had been a difficult three weeks. By the end a working if prickly relationship had emerged between old Chief Williams and herself, based on a grudging mutual respect.

Her role as pioneer boat crew Wren was leading to some interesting by-ways.

It had been a major disappointment to be taken off her Thames launch *Kittiwake* when her all-Wren crew were doing so well but the alternative challenges that were being assigned to her might make up for that. Jane thought back to her summons to headquarters. Her divisional officer Merle Baker had laid out the intended programme, emphasising that it had been drawn up at a much higher level than a mere third officer acting as the messenger. "First of all, we are sending you to Pompey for three weeks right away. They are being distinctly dubious about the idea of Wrens in boats and we'd like you to go and show them what you can do. You will be on their boats with an otherwise male crew, but we have arranged accommodation for you in the Petty Officer Wrens' block. Congratulations, incidentally, on your promotion. I had no idea that was coming until the chit landed on my desk.

Next, there is something completely different for you. We have been asked if Wrens could provide crews for barges working on the canals. Our director is rather taken with the idea but it seems that it is so completely a different world that we are uncertain. Therefore we have arranged for you to do a trip on one of them, from London to Birmingham and back. The canal you are going on is called the Grand Union Canal. The fleet of barges which run up and down on it transports mixed freight north, and southward brings coal from the Coventry coalfields to London. They are all owned by the same private company.

Most of these barges are run by families and one of them has a daughter your age for you to team up with. They are willing to have you providing you work with them and really get a feel for what is involved. We'll give you some cash and coupons to pay for your food. Once you have completed the trip we want a report from you detailing your experience and conclusions; you can draft it here at headquarters. "

Merle continued: "After that you are getting a little leave before going on a signals course from tenth August. That will last a month, then there may be one or two odd jobs to do before you go back to Plymouth in early October as part of the team preparing for the first boat crew Wrens' training course, starting in late October. Plans for this are still being finalised but we intend that you should be part of the training team which will otherwise be male Naval personnel. That's as far ahead as we have planned now but you may be quite sure there will be plenty for you to do. I've got this written out for you. Any questions?"

"Not so much questions as to tell you what I am doing, although this programme doesn't leave a lot of time for it. The main thing is that David and I are getting married in mid-September. His ship is expected to go back into service around the end of September so we want to get this in before he goes off to sea again. It's happening in the chapel at Hemel Towers and you are invited. Can you come?"

"Jane, that's wonderful. Of course I will come unless I get stuck by duty. Have you an actual date yet?"

"We're hoping for Saturday 20th but that isn't final yet. One other thing: is there any chance of *Kittiwake's* crew being allowed off to come too?"

"Can't promise it Jane but we'll see what we can do. There is a war on, I'm afraid."

"Do you have any plans for me beyond this training course?"

"No, that's too far ahead to be firmed up yet. Possibly stay on the training staff at Guzz, or go somewhere else to get Wren boat crews established. We'll see." So here she was, assignment one completed. This business of going on a barge for about three weeks might be very interesting; certainly very different and presumably not under usual Wren discipline.

Coming into Lady Ormond's flat was starting to feel a little like coming home despite its grandness. The lady's offer of her home to be used any time was generous and Jane was finding it extremely handy to have a base like this in London. She seemed as pleased as ever to see Jane, even if only for a few days. With Fiancé David away somewhere doing some rough shooting Jane relaxed, caught up with correspondence, and tried to find out about canals. There was not a lot she could find, other than a technical description of how a lock worked but at least she could make sense of that. She was ordered to find Bull's Bridge depot, at Southall, where apparently the barges moored up between trips. No-one at Headquarters had any real idea what she would need for working on a barge; all they knew was that space was severely limited so she took her inflatable mattress and a kitbag with everything else she might need, and set off for Southall. She was met at the station by a van driven by a silent bloke in overalls and deposited outside a works office. Stretching away were multiple boats, all moored stern to the quay. "You'll find the works manager in there. He'll tell you what to do."

CHAPTER TWO:
On Board

Enquiring around, Jane located the manager deep in discussion in a store full of ropes and pots and bits of machinery. She waited patiently until he had finished then introduced herself. "Ah, you're the Wren we have been expecting. Hmm. You look strong enough for the job, but are you really?"

"Hard to say until I try it but I'm pretty fit and strong. We'll just have to give it a go and see."

He smiled and escorted her into a dusty little office crammed with bits of equipment and piles of paper. "Now, let me give you a bit of a run-down on what you'll find yourself put into. These boats are called narrow boats, never barges and their crews will get very cross if you do call them barges so remember that. They are run by families most of whom have been on the cut for generations and they have their own very strict ways of behaving. Because the way of life is special they tend to marry among themselves and as a result it is a bit of a closed community. A young lady like you will have to be careful not to get too chatty with their young men. They are always on the move, which means that their courting is done in little snatches and in consequence small actions can assume large significance. Among these people a girl going to the cinema with one of their boys is a statement that they are committed to each other. So bear that in mind. The families are rather old-fashioned in that the husband who is known as the steerer is very much the captain and also head of the family. Certain jobs are strictly confined to one or other of the couple: shopping is always done by the wife, for example, and the man looks after the engine. But working the boats is done by everyone on board, including the little kids. You will have to find how you fit in to this but do not doubt or argue with the steerer."

Jane smiled gently. "Looks like I will have to mind my Ps and Qs pretty carefully then."

"Yes indeed. A couple of other points of etiquette before I introduce you to your family. One, it is the height of discourtesy to go onto someone else's boat without being invited. If you want to go aboard another one, knock on the cabin side and wait. That little cabin is their home, after all, and it is just like knocking on someone's front door. They are very hospitable but always on their own terms. And two, theirs is a hard life where money is scarce as they are paid by the cargo and not very much at that. I know the arrangement is that you will give the wife some money and coupons for your food but they are a proud people in their own way so try to avoid flaunting money at them. Any questions?"

"That's enough for now."

"Right, two more things before we go and meet your family. This is a windlass which works the paddle gear on the locks. Everyone has their own and this is for you while you are on the boat. Don't lose it whatever you do." And he handed over a right-angled metal handle with a square ring on one end. "The other thing is that you'll need a strong belt. Everyone wears one on the cut and with good reason; you'll do a lot of straining and heaving in the next few weeks." And he produced a broad leather belt.

"Good heavens, that's worse than a corset. What on earth do we do that needs something like that?"

"You'll find out soon enough but believe me, you will need it. I think probably best to go and meet your family now."

"All right, let's go."

They passed by the row of narrow boats, all lying with their sterns to the quay, smoke gently drifting from cabin chimneys and their crews looking on silently. There was something disconcerting about that silence; not hostile but cautious, withdrawn and wary of the intruder in their midst. The silence had an almost physical force. Arriving at a boat which to Jane looked like all the others, the manager said "Right this is it. These boats work in pairs; a motorboat and a butty which doesn't have an engine and gets towed behind. You will find that the couple whose boat this is, live on the motor and their daughter will be sharing the butty's cabin with you."

"How on earth do you tell them apart? They all look the same to me."

"Conveniently, they all have names. Here, if you look the butty is called *Endymion* and the motor is *Rome*. Your hosts, the Smythsons, have had this pair for years and brought up their family on them. Now there's just their youngest, Julie, still with them."

"Oh, did they have a large family then?"

"Yes, the narrow boat community tend to have substantial families, in part because the children are a working part of the business but don't get paid. In some ways how they operate has an almost Victorian feel to it."

"There can't be many ways of life left now in England where the children have to work for their living."

"Well no, but you will find a surprising amount of it lingers in little pockets like the boat people." He knocked on *Rome's* stern and an old man looked out. "'Ow do, Mr Woods, you've got the girl?"

"'Ow do Jake, Yes this is her. Can I bring her on board?"

"Yes, do." So they scrambled over the stern and Jane was ushered into the cabin where a large lady was sitting with a girl much the same age as Jane, beside her. The old lady's face was deeply tanned and lined, with a solid air as though carved from a piece of teak. She wore an elaborate bonnet with a frilled front to it, ribbons hanging down and a large flap at the back covering her neck. This was combined with a full-length black dress with a white apron over it. The girl had a light flowery summer frock on; she was equally tanned with a lean muscular air to her. The lady spoke in a deep booming voice which reverberated round the little cabin. "'Ello my dear, welcome to moi 'ome. I 'ope you'll be comfy with us. Moi Julie'll show yew the butty later. You're a good size; are yew as strong as you look?"

"I think so, Mrs Smythson, and pretty fit. I gather that is fairly important for working on these boats."

"So you are goin' to work? The other Navy bloke we got wouldn't do a 'and's turn. Said 'e was 'ere to hobserve and not be used as cheap labour."

"Well my instructions are to find out if Wrens could work on these boats and I don't see how I could do that without actually doing the work myself. Is it very hard?"

"Not to us it isn't but to a soft girl off the bank it might be a bit much. We'll see. Now, did you bring coupons and some money?"

"Yes, indeed." And Jane fished in her purse, handing over five pound notes and a ration book.

Mrs Smythson smiled. "That'll do us fer a woile. Julie, pop these 'ere in the key drawer." The girl did as she was told, putting the items in a small drawer tucked away in the bulkhead.

"Can yew cook?"

"No, I'm afraid not. I've always been where there were others for that."

"Never mind, I do it 'ere and moi Julie is pretty 'andy at it too. How will yew ever get a 'usband if you can't cook?"

"Well I'm engaged so getting a husband isn't a problem and I don't think an ability to cook is going to be very important."

"Engaged, eh? So you'll not be after our boys?"

Jane, remembering the caution from the manager, smiled gently and said "No, I shan't be chasing them."

"Good thing 'an all. Our Julie here is courtin' an' we don't want no messing about with her Jeb."

"Oh please Mrs Smythson, I'm not that stupid."

The lady smiled grimly and nodded. "Roight, Julie 'ere will show you the butty were you'll be sleepin'. Yew can unpack you stuff there. Yew did bring some workin' clothes with you, I 'ope?"

"Oh yes, I've got my boat rig with me. You can't do much on a boat in this tiddley uniform."

"They said sometin' about you bein' in boats. Yew works in them?"

"All the time. I've been running a launch on the Thames for the past six months and lots of other boat work before that."

Mrs Smythson nodded grimly before a smile broke the solidity of her face. "That moit help a bit though oi suspect you'll find this a bit different. Jane yew said your name was?"

Jane nodded.

"Roit Julie, show Jane 'ere the butty then come back 'ere for supper."

Jane turned to leave and found Mr Smythson in the hatchway. It was his turn to speak. "We'll be untying about six in the mornin'. Yew can coom wi' me on the motor to begin with. We're goin to Lime 'Ouse to load steel then down the cut to Tyseley. You'll know a bit about it by time we get there."

Jane almost replied 'Aye Aye sir' but checked herself and settled for "Yes, Mr Smythson." He clearly did not expect any other sort of response.

Julie slid the butty's hatch back and gestured to Jane to go in. "This'll be your 'ome wile you's with us. Did you bring your bed?"

"Yes, I've got my inflatable mattress and sleeping bag. That should do?"

"I ain't never seen a 'flatable mattress. Does it stay up?"

"Usually, yes. I gather we have to put the bedding away during the day."

"That's roit. But yew can blow it up each night. Put your stuff in those two drawers."

Jane unpacked, watched closely by Julie. "You've got an awful lot o' stuff. Is that everything you've got?"

Jane remembered the manager's warning about not flaunting wealth and smelt a trap. "No, there's a bit more back at base but I wasn't sure what I would need here so I've brought gear to cover different situations. We'll see what I really need." Jane had unpacked her concertina and laid it on the table.

"Do you play that thing? There's a few of the men play things like that."

"Oh yes, I play it. Would you like a tune?" Julie nodded enthusiastically, so Jane launched off into 'Green Sleeves'.

Tune played, Julie clapped. "That was lovely. You'll be real popular in the pubs of an evenin'."

"Oh, you stop and go into pubs in the evenings?"

"Wen we can, yes. We do terrible long hours but stop for a bit overnight 'cos yew can't run much after dark; they close the lock gates then."

"Oh, it will be interesting to go into the pubs then. I presume these are on the canal side and other boat crews go there too?"

"Yes, we have our own pubs right on the bank and you'll meet lots of other boat people. I'm hoping to see moi Jeb when we get to Stoke; 'e'll be in the pub there, the *Boat Inn,* in the evenin'.

"Now that will be interesting. Are you engaged?"

"Well we're courtin' an' we go out together wen we can. We're going to get proper married in a church next year. Wen you gettin' married?"

"We hope twentieth September but my fiancé is in the Navy and it depends on what happens with his ship."

"Moi brothers is in the Navy. They got called up an' are in destroyers."

"Oh, so is my fiancé. Maybe they will meet some day."

A bellow interrupted this chat. "That's ma sayin' supper's ready. Let's go an' get fed."

Supper proved to be two fried sausages, a slice of fried bread and a lump of something black which lurked on the plate. Black pudding, she was told. It proved to taste better than it looked and Jane was in her usual hungry state so ate it without hesitating. Ample tea washed this lot down. By the time they turned in Jane had been regaled with long family histories which she struggled to keep hold of. Cousins and aunts came and went; Jane got a feeling that beneath the 'head of the family' status of the elder men on the boats, the whole set-up was a matriarchy with women doing most of running the business. Certainly there was much less talk of male bloodlines.

Turning in, she asked Julie if she set an alarm for the early start. "No, oi always wakes up wen the daylight comes anyways."

"Fine, would you mind calling me as soon as you get up? I'll probably sleep longer if left."

* * *

The canals of England are a network of waterways linking the main industrial centres with ports and the sea. They were an essential precursor to the industrial revolution which swept Britain in the late eighteenth century and into the nineteenth. For about fifty years they were the primary arteries of freight and commerce, before being relegated by the coming of the railways. But they continued to serve a useful purpose, especially in carrying bulk goods like coal, with demand still substantial if slowly dwindling up to the Second World War. There was then a brief final flourishing as every means of transport capable of moving goods was pressed into action in the country's hour of need. There were two main areas: the northern canals served a sweep from Liverpool to Manchester and Yorkshire and with routes down through the Potteries to Birmingham. The southern part of the system linked London with Birmingham and the Midlands plus a route between Birmingham and the River Severn basin.

The most important canal was probably the Grand Union going north to Birmingham and Coventry from London. It had been redeveloped and improved between the two World Wars and carried a substantial traffic of piece goods like steel and Aluminium northbound, and coal south. The canal company owned a substantial fleet of narrow boats, run by the boat families. Early in the second war a manning crisis started to emerge. Just when their boats' carrying capacity was most needed, many of the younger men who were essential to the running of the boats, were called up into the armed services. This left the boats in the hands of older men, and of women who despite a lifetime's experience struggled to run boats on their own. Some managed, other left the boats to "go on the bank" as going to live ashore was called. This meant that just as they were most needed, narrow boats were being left abandoned and going nowhere.

This was the world that Jane was suddenly dropped into. The thinking was that if Wrens could supplement the crews more boats might be able to keep going. Jane had been despatched to see what this would involve, and report back.

CHAPTER THREE:
On The Move

It felt like only a few moments later that Julie was gently shaking Jane "Yew asked to be called. Time to get up."

Jane rolled over, scratched her head and groaned. "All right. What's the time?"

Julie shrugged. "Don't know clock time. Day's comin' in nicely."

A check told her five forty-five as she rolled out, pulled on bell bottoms, white front and an old jersey. "Do we breakfast now?"

"Naw. Once we're goin' I'll fix something."

Obediently she followed Julie over to the motor to find the Smythsons already untying. The motor slipped ahead and as it passed the butty Julie picked up a short rope from its bow which she turned up on a small cleat on the motor's stern.. As she did so Mrs Smythson stepped over onto the butty, walked to its after end and shipped the big tiller which had been turned up out of the way. Julie meantime had gone forward with a long pole which she put against the far bank and pushed hard. The butty followed along and the pair slipped out of the moorings without disturbing any of the other boats. Almost immediately Mr Smythson turned hard to starboard (the right) to go under a white painted bridge over a canal arm leading off at a right angle. All this happened so quickly and neatly that Jane was hard put to follow what was going on. Once round Julie came aft and said " 'Ere, grab that short strap to cross with the one that's on, an' tie it onto that other stud." Jane looked confused. "Strap? I don't see any leather."

"Naw, that rope there. All our ropes is straps."

"Oh, right." It was dawning on Jane that not only was she going into a new way of life but would have to learn a whole new language as well. But the way they had slipped out of the moorings had been impressively neat boat handling. Mr Smythson looked at her closely. "Let's see how you steer. Yew all right steerin'?"

Jane had a wry smile to herself. She thought 'You should try a sailing boat with too much canvas on in a rising gale' but contented herself with saying. "Oh yes, I can steer. From what I read, the pivot point is about one third along from the bow?"

"Pivot point? How'd you mean, Jane?"

"That's the point in the length of the boat about which it turns."

"Don't know about no pivot point. She just goes round the corners. Good steerer, this one. She swims nicely too wich is wy we've stayed in her 'though she's gettin' old."

She thought, 'All right Jane, don't get smart aleck with these people. They probably know their business in a practical way to leave me right behind.'

"All right, yew take the elum." And he handed the tiller over. "We've got a couple of hours of this pound so you've got time to get used to her."

Jane nodded and settled to getting to know this long thin boat with another one tied close behind. The canal passed through industrial areas, then housing, interspersed with open country. After some initial experimenting Jane found the boat easy to steer if a little slow to respond but that seemed to be the effect of the butty, tied close astern, pulling on the motor's stern until it also started to turn. Julie suddenly popped her head out of the motor's cabin. " 'ere's yer breakfast" two sausages and a slice of toast came up along with a large mug of tea. Mr Smythson stayed on the side of the cabin, keeping an eye on things as gradually the landscape become fully urban. The canal was busy, with much wider barges passing by, mostly towed by large horses. "Keep to the outside" ordered Mr Smythson.

"Outside?" queried Jane.

"Yeah, away from the tow ropes."

"Oh, right" she acknowledged. It was logical but not something she would have thought of. Overbridges were becoming more frequent and as they approached another one half a dozen children were lined up. Mr Smythson grunted, pulled his hat down over his brow and hunched his shoulders. As they passed under the children screamed "Filthy gypsies, filthy gypsies" and threw stones at the boat then spat on the steerers as they passed under. Jane was livid. "Good God, why do you put up with that?" Her captain shrugged. "Not much yew can do about it. If yer try chasin' 'em they'll be gone afore yew gets near 'em. That's life fer boaters." And he gloomily pulled his hat closer over his face. Jane shook her head in impotent fury. "That really is wrong. Something should be done about it." But Mr S just shrugged again. Ahead the canal divided "Go left, that's Paddington basin on the right." A tunnel entrance showed ahead. " 'Ere, I'll take her fer the tunnel. Yew watch wat I do." He steered close to the right hand wall of the brief tunnel then handed the tiller back to Jane. Next was pretty parkland scenery "Is this Regent's Park?"

Mr S gave a slightly sour smile and nodded. "Too many people. We'll be comin' to the first locks soon. Julie will lock-wheel them fer us. Yew go with 'er an' see what she does."

"Lock wheel? What's that?"

"Gettin' the lock ready for us."

"Oh, it needs preparing, does it?"

"Needs to be at our level and gates open."

Jane nodded. Again, the logic of it was obvious but not something she would have thought of. "Off at next bridge cut" ordered Mr S, taking the tiller. "Just step off as we go through." Jane transferred to the towpath as directed and stood, uncertain of what to do next. As the butty passed through, Julie stepped off and waved to Jane to follow. "Got yer windlass?"

"No, what do I need that for?"

"Working the locks, o' course. Yew'll need it."

A large barge was leaving the lock, its horse straining on the tow line, so the lock was ready for the narrow pair. As the motor entered the lock Mr S threw off the butty's short tow lines and steered over to the left side of the lock pit. Mrs S steered the butty in beside the motor, handed Julie a short hemp rope with which Julie took a couple of turns on a convenient bollard. Checking the butty's movement until it stopped alongside the motor, she then tossed the hemp rope back on board and took a clean white rope to the next bollard along. This was done with such neat precision that it barely registered. 'Nice boat handling' thought Jane. Immediately Julie put her back to the balance beam of the open gate, pushing it shut, ran round and closed the other one then whipped out her windlass. Now Jane saw what it was for, fitting over the square boss of a ratchet gear which Julie wound up vigorously. The boats started to drop down in the lock and with four of the ratchet gears wound up, Julie relaxed. "That gear operates the paddles to let water in – or out" she explained. "Yew go and open the lower gate when we're level down."

Jane crossed over and pushed but the gate was immoveably shut. "Wait fer it" called Julie. "Watch me." Jane leant against balance beam and suddenly felt it go light and to move. Imitating Julie she put her back to it and pushed but now it came readily. Meantime Julie dropped the paddles she had opened and as the boats cleared the lock called over "Shut the gate again, then get to the next lock." Obediently Jane pushed then trotted the hundred yards to the next lock. The procedure was the same and quickly Jane saw that going through a lock was a series of choreographed procedures. While they were waiting for the lock to drop Julie remarked "We allus leave the lock ready. There's one more lock fer now then yew can go back on the motor." Back on the motor Jane was handed the tiller again. "Take the elum" she was commanded. Meantime Julie had picked up the bicycle Jane had noted on the foredeck and peddled off down the towpath "She'll wheel the next lock then come through the tunnel with us. Yew stick here an' learn to steer into a lock." Jane headed into the lock close to the left hand side. With the butty tied alongside the pair filled the lock and again their progress was checked by Julie taking turns on the short hemp rope. "We keeps it for that job" remarked Mr S. They moved out of the lock and dropped the butty behind close to the motor as before, Mr S going through the same procedure of casually picking up a short line on the butty's foredeck as they passed by and turning it up on the motor's stud. At the next bridge hole Julie with bicycle stepped on board the butty and lit a lamp on its fore end. "We're better singled up fer the tunnel" explained Mr S. Ahead Jane could see another tunnel entrance. "Yew watch what I do".

This tunnel looked dark and impenetrable. "Is it longer?" she enquired.

Mr S nodded "A bit." He blew on a horn as they approached the entrance and from deep inside came an answering blast. "That's another narrow boat so we can go in. We'll pass him inside. Keep yer 'ands inside the boat wile we're in the tunnel."

The tunnel swallowed them, the only light now the weak beam of the headlight Mr S had switched on. Abruptly the engine exhaust, usually a gently popping chug ahead of them, came echoing back very loudly, bouncing off the roof of the tunnel and onto the people. Mr S kept the boat over close to the right hand wall, just a foot or two away from it. Suddenly this all felt very unnatural to Jane. Here was a boat, a creature of the open air and blue sky, chugging along too close to the brickwork side wall for comfort, engulfed in darkness and the earth above them. This was no place for a boat, Jane thought, but here they were. She was reminded of the Styx and the crossing into Hades. Out of the darkness another narrow boat loomed up, passing down their left hand side only a foot or so away. Nothing was said as they passed the other steerer and as suddenly as it had appeared it vanished and the blackness swallowed them again. Jane had never thought of herself being claustrophobic but there was something oppressive and unnatural about being on a boat in this deep darkness with just the wall of the tunnel sliding past close by as a marker of a solid world around them. Slowly light from the far end grew larger and it was with some relief that Jane screwed her eyes up against full daylight again. Within a few hundred yards they were at the next lock and again Julie stepped off. This lock was against them, emptied out and gates closed. This time Jane remembered her windlass and imitating Julie wound two of the ratchet gear paddles open. In no time the lock was full, so the paddles were dropped and the gates pushed open. The same neat boat handling followed for the boats entering the locks. The gates were pushed closed and the lock emptied. Julie peddled off to the next lock; from then on locks seem to come frequently and Jane found herself struggling to keep pace with the frequent activity. Abruptly over the next lock she could see a dock with ships in it and beyond that the Thames: she had a sudden spasm of longing to be on the tideway again with her *Kittiwakes,* where she knew what she was doing.

"Lime 'ouse" muttered Mr S.

"Oh, is this where we stop to load?"

Mr S grunted a nod. The dock was full of barges and sea-going ships with cranes moving cargoes around. There were a good few narrow boats tied up already, some loaded and being prepared to go, other busily receiving their cargoes, yet others sitting waiting. Everywhere there were men shouting, boats moving and an intense bustle to the place. Mr S tied his pair up outside several more pairs of narrow boats, the steerers gruffly acknowledging the new arrivals, the wives smiling and chatting even as they went about their chores. It struck Jane that these canal boat wives never stopped, they always had something in their hands and even when chatting from boat to boat they were polishing or knitting or peeling potatoes. There were little children running about, miraculously staying safe in the rowdy activity around them. Jane turned to Mrs S, "Are these kids off the narrow boats?"

"Yes dearie, we's all family boats and that means the little ones come with us. I've 'ad six children, y'know, four boys and two girls, all of 'em born on this boat but just Julie left with us. When she gets married next year we'll probably go on the bank 'cos running a pair two-handed is real 'ard work. My boys have all been called up an' are in the Navy but we'll see my Suey up the cut somewhere. She's married to a number one with three little ones of her own."

"What's a number one? Something special?"

"Kind of, it means he owns his own boat. Most of us just 'as a company boat."

Jane was getting really interested in this conversation when Mr S re-appeared having collected his orders from the dock office. "We'll be loaded tomorrow morning straight out of that Greek over there – steel bar. Should be out of here early afternoon an' I won't be sorry."

"Oh, why the hurry?"

"Bombs. They're not coming every night now but still have a go every now and then an' this dock is so crowded that a bomb in it can do a lot of damage. Have yew been bombed?"

"Oh yes, Stukas and hit-and-run and was under the blitz here. That's where I got my scars from."

"So you'll know why we want to get out of here. It's quieter in the countryside." Jane just smiled.

Julie stuck her head out of the butty's cabin. "Supper time. Come and get it."

Supper proved to be a brown stew with potatoes and carrots with yet another large mug of tea. Jane hadn't thought about food all day but the sudden sight of a plateful of stew set her salivating. They squeezed in round the butty's table with Mr S given the head of the table to himself while the women fitted in as they could. Julie settled on the coal box lid with her plate in her lap. Jane noted that Mr Smythson's plate was piled up until he said "That'll do" then the women had to share out what was left. It made for a noticeably smaller plateful, which struck Jane as a little unfair given that the women had worked just as hard physically through the day. But they behaved as though it was the natural order of things, so Jane took her share without comment. This was indeed a different world.

After supper the Smythsons washed faces, changed and smartened up and asked Jane, "We're going to the pictures. Do you want to come?"

"No thanks, I've letters to write and I could do with some time just to unwind."

"All right, see you later." Alone in the butty's cabin she settled down and must have dozed off for suddenly she was jerked awake by an almighty crash and the boat rocking violently. Dashing into the cockpit she saw chaos around her. Boats and barges adrift, one barge loaded with timber burning fiercely, and a narrow boat pair sinking slowly. Her pair were drifting slowly across the dock, the mooring ropes snapped. On the sinking narrow boat a man waved wildly for help. Looking around, Jane saw that she was nearest, perhaps twenty feet away. She grabbed one of the broken mooring ropes and heaved it with all her strength. Mercifully it reached over to be seized and pulled. Coming alongside the stricken boat, "Quickly now" she shouted. Three little children erupted from the cabin; in quick succession she pushed them into her butty's cabin, followed by the man. "Where's your wife?"

"Just comin', I think. Come on, Gladys."

A second later Gladys emerged clutching a sewing machine, a bag full of plates, brass knobs and important documents, and another with groceries in it. These precious items transferred, Gladys stepped over as the boat stood on its nose and slipped beneath the surface. Around them was a chaos of drifting boats, drifting timber and the odd crate, filling the dock basin.

"Where's Jake?" Bellowed the man she had rescued.

"They've all gone to the pictures. I'm alone here."

The man looked at Jane closely. "You're not one of us, what yew doin' here?"

"I'm a Wren, sent by the Navy to see what you people do."

"Ah, you're the Navy girl Jake's taken on. Done this before, 'ave yew?"

"Once or twice. Bloody Boche. Come on, let's get ourselves sorted out. Have you lost both your boats?"

"Afraid so. Motor went straight down then you saw what happened to the butty. We was loaded, too."

"Could you start our motor?"

"It'll take a few minutes but yes, oi can do that."

"Let's do it then. We'll have control with the engine running." Most of the other boats had nobody on board, their crews gone ashore like the Smythsons. Five minutes later *Rome's* engine coughed into life, Jane shipped her tiller and they set about collecting drifting pairs, tying them up in tiers. Quite unthinkingly Jane had taken charge of this, handling the motor, tying up boats and giving orders to her newfound motorman. A group of boat people had arrived on the quayside and as their boats were brought in they scrambled down and aboard. Last to come were the Smythsons. She shouted to Mr S, "Grab a line. We'll lie outside the other boats in this tier."

He waved acknowledgement and his boats were secured as well. Emergency over, he came on board and looked closely at Jane, black of face and wild of hair. The boat man she had rescued joined them. "Evenin' Jake. Your Navy girl is summat special. Bin telling us all wat ter do."

"I saw." He turned to Jane. "Yew've done this before, 'aven't you?"

"Well never on one of these boats but out on the river, yes I have."

Mr S smiled at this and turned to his wife. "Rose, how about gettin' the kettle on?" She went into the cabin to be confronted by the wife from the sunken boat and three small children. " 'Ello, Gladys. Lost your boat then?"

"Yeah. The bomb landed in the dock right agen us and blew 'em both to bits. We was lucky to get out alive. That Navy girl of yours is quite somethin'. My Joe don't usually take orders from no woman but she had him doin' just wat she wanted. Knew how to, too."

Mugs of tea were handed round then they debated what to do for Joe and his family now they had nowhere to go. With so little space available in a narrow boat's cabin they could not all be accommodated in any one boat. Jane listening to the debate, asked "Why not distribute you round the boats? Surely you people know each other well enough to accommodate one each in your boats?"

There was a rumble of agreement and the women fell to deciding who would go where. The eldest of the children, a girl of around eight years old, stayed in *Endymion* and Julie saw her settled. "Will we be together again termorrer?" was the girl's only concern.

"Yes of course Rosie, yew'll be together in a new boat in no time."

"That's all right then." And secure in the enveloping warmth of her people, she was asleep in moments.

CHAPTER FOUR:
Heading North

Early starts were nothing new to Jane but she had never liked them. So when her alarm went off at 0600 enthusiasm was lacking. Rolling out she noted that Julie was missing, and her bedding neatly rolled up. Dressing hastily and looking out of the hatch she saw that her boats were on the move already, slipping quietly over to berth outboard of a ship across the dock. Mr S smiled at her "Mornin'. We'll be loading soon."

"You should have called me, I'd have helped with tying up."

"That's all right, we can manage."

"Yes I know that but I'm here to be involved in everything you do. Please keep me doing what you do."

Mr. S smiled sourly, "Yew any good at catchin' rabbits?"

Startled, Jane shook her head, "Never tried that. Would that be for the pot?"

"Yeah, there's one or two spots where they're good 'n fat. Makes a nice supper."

They had been standing by the motor's hatch facing aft when suddenly the boat rolled to port. The first of the cargo had been landed in the hold. Mr S jumped onto the cabin roof and went forward, waving to Jane to follow. "Got ter keep an eye on them, ter make sure they put it in proper." Jane watched fascinated as sling after sling of steel bar was landed neatly in place in first the motor then the butty's hold. An hour and a half later both boats were loaded down with only a couple of inches of freeboard. Jane eyed this with some concern. "Aren't we a bit deep? The slightest wave would sink us, wouldn't?"

"Don't get waves in the cut. The water don't move, y'know."

"Oh all right, you know about it but you couldn't go on the river like this."

"But we ain't goin' on the river, so we's all right."

All Jane could do was shrug and hope that he really did mean what he said.

"We'll move out of the basin here, go up the first few locks then stop to put her together and sheet up. Don't want to be hangin' about here in case the Jerries come back. We'll be goin' up the locks so yew can try that with Julie."

"Oh, is going up the locks different?"

"A bit. Yew'll see. If we go now we'll get a good road."

Mr S rapped on the cabin roof. "We're goin'. Julie, take Jane an' show her how to work locks going up."

Julie waved to Jane to follow to the bow. They untied from the cargo ship, turned and as the pair came to the lock Julie jumped ashore motioning Jane to follow. The boats entered the lock pit breasted up and Mrs S handed the strap to Julie to check the butty's way. So far, so familiar, thought Jane. Julie meantime had run round to the other side of the lock and as soon as the pair were in the lock she pushed on the lower gate balance beam, waving to Jane to do the same. Jane had remembered her windlass this time and following Julie's lead opened the paddle gear to let water into the lock from the higher end. Jane had been warned to only lift the paddle half way at first or the boat could get swamped but even so there was a powerful blast of water. The boats rose up in a few minutes; Julie waved to Jane to push her gate open then let go the mooring ropes. Freed, Mr S pushed the other gate open with the motor's bow and revved up to clear the lock. Jane was beginning to see why the boats had heavy rope fenders on bow and stern; they were as much a part of working the boats as were the mooring ropes. The next lock was a repeat and Jane was seeing the same choreographed actions through each one. Just after lock six Mr S stopped his boats by the entrance to a side basin. "We'll tie up 'ere and sheet up."

"Sheet up? What's that?"

"Coom with me an' see."

Jane had noticed tarpaulins neatly rolled up along the sides of both boats. Now she found out what they were for as they were unrolled and strings from their upper edge were passed over the central plank then tied off. "Get 'em good an' tight," She was instructed. Working her way along she found one string with its splice coming loose so she hastily put a back splice into it then carried on down the side. "Yew've done that afore an' all."

"Well yes, I am a boat crew Wren. It's the kind of thing we do all the time."

Mr S merely smiled and grunted.

With the motor's cloths pulled up they transferred to the butty and did it all again. "Roit, now the top cloths." From the fore end a loose tarpaulin was put on the walkway plank and unrolled, its sides falling over the stretched side cloths. Strings from its edges tied off on the boat's sides pulling the top cloths tight, and the cargo was completely covered over. With both boats dealt with Mr S relaxed. "Usually we'd do this where we loaded but I 'ate 'anging about at Lime 'ouse so I cooms up 'ere instead. We'll get goin' again as soon as missus comes back. Now 'ow about yew putting the kettle on?"

Jane smiled agreement. It was clear that in Mr Smythson's world all women were expected to do domestic chores; this might seem old-fashioned to Jane but she saw no point in arguing. She stirred up the coal in the stove, filled the kettle from the water can sitting on the cabin roof and five minutes later had the teapot filled. It was as well that she had filled the large teapot as Mrs Smythson and Julie returned with bags filled with groceries and were glad of the cuppa. "There's a good shop 'ere wat knows about us boat people an' lets us 'ave some special bits froom under the counter. We'll feed well this trip."

Mr S in the meantime had disappeared into the engine room and soon the gentle if uneven chug of the Bolinder was vibrating through the boat. Emerging, Mr S called "Roit, got to get ahead so untie her. Jane, we'll need to single out so yew take the motor an' Julie the butty." Within minutes the mouth of Islington tunnel loomed up and Jane, remembering her sense of discomfort last time, shivered gently. "Are you going to take her through?" she asked Mr. S.

"No, yew can do it. Just keep to the roit hand side, close to the wall but don't bump it." An unaccustomed sense of panic gripped Jane; somehow this tunnel was an alien world and she felt scared in it. But 'I will not be defeated' came into her mind as the bow was swallowed up, and clutching the tiller tightly she steered over close to the right-hand side, picked up by the boat's searchlight. After this panicky surge the actual trip through was an anti-climax, the boat more or less steering itself with just the lightest of touches needed to keep it close by the wall. But emerging into the daylight again was a welcome relief and the approving nod from Mr S some comfort. Past Regent's Park and a few more locks, Mr S grunted "Roit, it's all flat now to the depot so we'll let the butty out to the end of the snubber an' keep goin'". Jane watched with interest as the tow rope was lengthened from the butty until it was a full boat's length astern and the two boats could be steered separately.

Dusk was falling as the snubber line was shortened in, they passed under the whitewashed Bull's Bridge which Jane recognised and Mr S put the boats alongside the depot quay with his usual skill. For the past half hour the smell of cooking meat had been reminding Jane of her stomach and she was delighted to be called in by Mrs S to a repeat of the previous evening meal. Mr S had his plate piled up until he said stop, then what was left was divided between the three women. Jane could have managed more than she got but her portion proved very tasty and just about sufficed. Mr S wandered off to talk some other boatmen, Julie set about washing up and Mrs S smiled at Jane. "Our Julie tells me yew play a squeezebox. Would yew play somethin' fer me?"

"Yes, sure. I'll just get it." And for over an hour she played simple dance tunes which seemed to please her audience. She had not noticed Mr S coming back until he spoke from the hatchway. "That'll go down well in the *Boat.*"

"Oh, where is that?"

"The pub at Stoke Bruin where we'll be seein' Julie's Jeb an' maybe our Suey too."

"Is that tomorrow?"

"Naw, two days to Stoke. Yew will see soon enough."

It did not feel as though she had been asleep for two minutes before Jane felt a gentle hand on her shoulder. "Daylight's just comin' in. We'll be off in ten minutes."

Jane grunted and rolled out. Julie smiled at her as she quickly put on her boat clothes again and rolled up her bedding. "Lots of locks for us today. Yew'll be good at them 'afore we're done. Remember to put your belt on, yew will need it today." And with that warning Julie shot out the hatch just as the engine fired on the motor boat. Hastily climbing out Jane was in time to see them arranging a long rope through loops on the butty's walkway and its end tied off on the after end of the motor. Mrs S took her place at the butty's elum and as the motor pulled away she slowly let out the snubber rope to its full length. They were on their way to Birmingham.

* * *

The Grand Union Canal is the primary water artery between London and the Midlands. It was an amalgamation of independent canals brought together under one ownership and developed with better locks in the 1930's. It still had substantial freight traffic on it which had been slowly reducing under competition from rail and road. But general goods, bulk items like steel and aluminium ingots and southbound a large coal trade kept the canal busy. This slow decline was halted by the Second World War when every possible means of transport was pressed into use again. The main delivery area was Birmingham but Coventry, Leicester and Northampton all had substantial traffic to them as well. The route climbed over the Chilterns, but then fell and rose again several times along its length. Pairs of narrow boats, a motorised one with an unpowered butty towed behind moved between fifty and sixty tons of freight at a time. The Grand Union owned a fleet of narrow boats but independent narrow boat companies still flourished and a number of the traditional owner skippers, often known as Number Ones, still operated their own boats although the tough times of the 1930's depression had winnowed out many of them. The Second World War gave them all a final flourish before the post war need for haste slowly drained away the last of their trade.

* * *

To begin with they were passing factories and industrial scenery, some with narrow boats tied up to them, discharging coal. Julie was on the motor's elum while Mr S disappeared into the engine room. Jane was left perched on the side of the motor's cabin watching as they settled to their journey. It wasn't long before the first lock loomed up in front of them. They had a good road, with the locks open for them to go straight into, and Jane followed Julie in stepping off at a bridge hole just before it. Motor and butty slipped in to the lock in their usual neat way and Julie gestured to Jane to push her gate shut. Then it was out with her nice new windlass, open the paddles and watch the boats rise up. In less than five minutes they were on their way again. The girls stepped onto the boat for the five minute ride to the next lock before repeating the choreographed performance. Once through that lock Julie remarked, "The next lock is the deepest on this cut. Don't fall over in it."

The warning was well meant, Jane finding its extra depth disconcerting but it functioned as the others did, give or take heavier gates to shut which called for most of Jane's strength. With Denham Deep lock behind them they settled to a rhythm of a lock about every five minutes, just long enough between them to justify hitching a ride on board and having a brief rest. They passed through a mix of countryside and residential areas with a series of reservoir lakes on the west side of the canal, and Jane was finding this rather pleasant. But this rhythm did not last. Two locks came together and after that they seemed to come in ever quicker succession with just long enough to trot from one to the next before the boats arrived. They were now in countryside and the sense of open space felt good to Jane; a lot of the locks were very pretty and some absolutely beautiful, set in deeply rural surroundings which pressed in round them. Appreciating this was a matter of a snatched minute or two while the lock was filling then it was into action again. Despite the sense of rural spaciousness towns passed by as did factories, each with a quay face on the canal at which narrow boats were discharging coal.

Through the day she lost all sense of time or distance; life was reduced to the next lock and keeping on the move. Sometime during the day they passed by Hemel Hempstead and Jane had a wry smile, reflecting on the very different lifestyle she knew just a few miles away. But not for long: the next lock came looming up and it was out with the windlass again. By some time in late afternoon, with locks still in front of them, Jane was feeling very weary, her back ached and she now saw why the belts were worn. Julie, she noticed, seemed unbothered by this constant working through locks. In a summer frock but with her broad leather belt and heavy boots on, she looked a bit incongruous but evidently the outfit suited the job. She certainly was not getting hot and sweaty the way Jane was. By early evening Jane was feeling every muscle when Julie suddenly called "This is Cow Roast lock an' we're finished with goin' up. We'll stop agen here till the morning."

'Well thank goodness' thought Jane. 'I've had enough.'

They tied up just outside the lock and Mr S disappeared into an office on the far bank. He came back fifteen minutes later with a thunderous face. "We've been told ter take the Bottom Road to the pits. I tried to tell 'em it was no good but they said we must ter save water. "Mr Smythson, they says, Mr Smythson there's a war on and we have ter rationalise how we do things, including economising on water. Rationalise! I'll give 'em rationalise. God I 'ates bein' told what ter do."

Both Mrs S and Julie had groaned at this announcement. All this puzzled Jane.

"Do you get orders here, and what's this about the Bottom Road?"

"Yeah that there is the traffic hoffice. Afore the war they just told us what the next cargo was then we was free to get it any way we wanted. Now they seems ter think they can tell us what ter do the 'ole time. I'm a boatman, a captain from a boating family what's been up an' down this cut for nigh on forty years an' never failed to deliver, yet these hoffice types sittin' at their desks seems to think they know more an' can tell me wat ter do. An' the Bottom Road is 'orrible; it's a dirty, long slow way round an' all single locks so yew 'as to bowhaul the butty. That's real 'ard work. I 'ate it, I 'ate it." Jane had not seen Mr S getting emotional about anything but this clearly upset him deeply so she decided not to ask further questions. He sat at the table glowering into the distance but Jane couldn't help noticing that his appetite was unaffected. Given that Julie and she had done the hard work during the day while he just stood steering the motor it seemed a bit unfair that Mr S got his usual large helping with a good deal less for the three women, but Julie and Mrs S seemed to regard this as normal so Jane decided just to take what she was given. There was bread on the table and some spare gravy in the pot so she dipped the bread in and filled up with that. After supper Mr S disappeared onto the bank saying nothing. In the butty's warm cabin Jane struggled to stay awake; even blowing up her mattress was hard work but her weary body welcomed it and in moments she sank into deep oblivion.

Again it was Julie gently shaking her shoulder that dragged Jane up to the surface. "Day's comin' in nicely an' we'll be goin' in a few minutes. Yew joinin' us?"

"Yes of course. Give me a minute." But she felt every muscle in her body as she rolled out stiffly, aching and unwilling. As she put her head out of the hatch she saw Mr S coming on board with a couple of rabbits in his hand. He went straight into the engine room and started the engine. Giving it a minute to settle to its rhythm he nodded to let go. The boats were now on the summit level of the trip over the Chilterns but not for long, so they stayed breasted up. Tring summit level is largely in a deep cutting; this was another new experience for Jane who again got that oppressed feeling she got in the tunnel. But it was verdantly beautiful in the gentle dawn light which dispersed the overbearing sense of being set deep in the earth. Half an hour brought them to the top lock and Mr S tied the boats up just short of it. "This 'ere's Maffers an' I got somethin' ter show yew," he said enigmatically to Jane and led her a short way along the towpath. He gently pulled open a large workshop door and beckoned her inside. Here were lock gates in various stages of construction, racks of timber up to very large tree trunks and a good deal of woodworking machinery. "They makes gates for most of the cut round 'ere," Mr S remarked. "I thought it moit interest yew ter see 'em bein' made." And indeed Jane was fascinated. Only here, laid out on trestles, was it clear how massive these gates were. For ten minutes she happily immersed herself in looking around; at their early hour none of the workmen were in so she could go as she pleased. "Well, got to get ahead," Mr S said. "Seen enuff?"

Jane nodded happily and a couple of minutes later was back in the locking routine. This time they were going down so she watched Julie and followed her movements just to make sure she got it right. Seven locks later they took the right hand cut away from the Alesbury branch and soon they were at another two locks. Mr S seemed in a more relaxed, almost jovial mood and smiled as he said " 'ere, it's time moi bestmate did some work. She can show you how to steer the butty an' work the snubber. There's not so many locks now."

"Don't you need me for the locks?" She queried.

"Naw, Julie can manage an' moi bestmate can join 'er. Yew learn to steer the butty."

So she joined Mrs S in the butty's steering well. Mr S pulled ahead on the motor and as soon as the butty was clear of the lock Mrs S started letting out the snubber line, paying it out over a small cleat on the cabin roof. "Yew 'as to mind yews fingers doin' this" she cautioned. "It's real easy to get 'em trapped on the stud, specially if the snubber tightens sudden loik."

Round a couple of bends and they came to the next lock. Julie stepped on to the bank, Mrs S took in the slack of the snubber as the motor entered the lock then stepped ashore herself taking the checking strap with her. Jane managed to steer the butty into its place and as Mrs S took a couple of turns on a strapping post the butty eased to a halt. Jane heaved up the cotton line to tie the boat up. Mrs S effortlessly pushed the gate shut and producing her windlass from somewhere in her voluminous dress opened the paddles to let the water out of the lock. Bottom gates open, Mr S went ahead slowly to let the two on the lock reboard their boats. It all looked effortless with exact timing of each movement leading to the next one. As they pulled away Mrs S said "Let the snubber out easy as it pulls away. Allus keep a turn on the stud so yew can control the line but mind yews fingers."

This was logical to Jane, thinking that the rope handling was just as she would have done it in a launch. They were now in totally rural country with barely a sign of human habitation. "We calls this bit 'the fields'" confided Mrs S. "Pretty isn't it?" Jane smiled agreement. Single locks passed by at intervals, the same neatly choreographed movements taking the boats through with minimum fuss. The canal seemed to have become much more twisty with a succession of sharp double bends. Leighton Buzzard passed by then they were in deep countryside again. After the previous day's frantic and constant toil this was rather pleasant. "Yew strove well yesterday" remarked Mrs S "this is easier."

Jane smiled agreement and concentrated on keeping the butty exactly behind the motor. Through the continuous twists and turns of the canal she found she had to keep her wits about her; pleasant though the surroundings were there was little enough time to relax and absorb them. After passing through a set of three locks there was a long level length. "Just keep followin' the motor an' you'll be foin," said Mrs S. She had collected the rabbits from their hiding place in the engine room and settled to skinning and cleaning them with skilled expertise. "We'll eat well tonight" she confided to Jane.

Another lock came up ahead of them, but there was something odd about it; the water level looked the same on both sides. "Oh, this is Fenney," said Mrs S. "We'll go down about a foot."

"Why did they bother with it?"

Mrs S shrugged. "Somethin' to do wiv breaking up the length of the pound. Don't really know."

"A bit different from Denham deep."

"Those old navvies had to take it as it came." This meant more wiggles, sharp corner after sharp corner with no straights at all. Suddenly round a corner a long narrow straight showed up; there was something odd about it. "Mrs S, what's this we are coming to?"

The lady stuck her head up from the cabin. "Ah, that's the pig trough ackeyduck. Just keep goin' straight behind the motor."

It proved to be an aqueduct and suddenly Jane found herself thirty feet in the air in what seemed like a very flimsy trough, giving her the feeling that if the boat bashed it hard enough it would just give way. But its wrought iron construction had withstood a hundred and fifty years of constant traffic so it had to be stronger than it looked. 'Well well, sometimes we're in the depths of the earth, sometimes up in the air. Going on a canal is certainly different.' She thought, 'You do get all sorts of varied textures of the land like this.' At the far end was yet another lock then it was settling down to endless bends again through deep countryside with neither road nor rail near them. The peace of it was profound. It was late afternoon when the next locks appeared. Mrs S looked up from the cabin. "Oh good, Stoke locks at last. We're nearly there." An hour later they were out of the top lock and into a lively community atmosphere.

CHAPTER FIVE:

Canal People

There was a row of narrow boats tied up at Stoke Bruerne; one was a bit special. Mrs S showed some excitement for the first time since Jane had come on board. "Oh look, she's here!"

"Who, Mrs S?"

"Suey my eldest daughter, and the little ones." On cue three small children, jumping up and down with excitement, tumbled out of a breasted-up butty's cabin. "Hello Granny, hello Granny," they all shrilled. Mrs. S's solid impassive face was split by the widest beam, a revelation to Jane of a different person. Before the arriving boats were tied up Mrs S had stepped across and was hugging the children; a statuesque woman emerged to join the embrace.

Jane, tying up *Rome,* looked at Mr S, "Don't you join in this?"

He shrugged, "Good to see my family goin' strong, but little ones is women's business. When they're big enough to be useful I takes 'em in hand an' makes boaters of 'em."

"Do all the boat family heads behave like you?"

"They used to but some of the younger ones is goin' soft with dads doin' things with the babies. That'll be the end of boating families, mark my word. Head of family must lead an' be in charge, not be messing about with little ones." And Mr S lapsed into gloomy silence. Julie had joined them and said "Jane, come on over an' meet me sister. She's heard all about yew an' is real curious." Meeting Suey, Jane was struck by how like her mother she was. A large lady who could not have been more than thirty or so, but had the same lined teak block face. Julie still had the prettiness of youth but the family likeness was clear and doubtless she would go the same way as hard work, childbirth and a life in the open air took their toll. These people really were a tribe on their own, reflected Jane, harnessed to an all-engrossing way of life, yet they seemed happy with it. "Yew 's all coming to eat rabbit stew," announced Mrs S. Two families squashed into one butty cabin left no space at all so Mr S and Suey's husband Bill stayed outside with a large jug of beer and had platefuls handed up to them. Jane squeezed onto the side bed, where a small girl parked herself on her lap and announced "I'm Lizer. What's yew called?"

"I'm Jane."

"Is yew comin' off the bank to be with us?"

"For now yes, but not permanently. How old are you, Lizer?"

Lizer shook her head. "Don't know. How old is old?"

Suey called across the cabin "She's three."

Jane's turn came and a plateful of the rabbit stew was handed to her with a fork and a spoon. Sitting with little Lizer on her knee made eating awkward but the girl obviously thought this natural. She grabbed the spoon and helped herself from Jane's plateful. Looking round the cabin Jane saw the other little ones also on knees and eating from their adult's plate so again she made a rapid adjustment to her expectations of good manners and ate from the plate. Lizer had a good appetite and not for the first time Jane was left with a feeling that she could have managed more but the pot was empty. The women of the family were deeply engrossed in chat about other members of the family so Jane wiped Lizer's mouth with her hankie, smiled at her and said, "Do you want to go and play?"

Lizer shook her head, "It's nice here. Can I stay?"

Small children were not something Jane knew much about in any practical way so relying on instinct she gave the tot a hug and said, "Certainly, if you want."

Lizer snuggled round a bit and settled down; within minutes she was sleeping peacefully leaving Jane stuck in her corner. There was something oddly comforting about this bundle of warmth's complete trust. But warm it was: the atmosphere in the cabin was hot and stuffy and having a small child cuddled up in her lap, Jane got very hot indeed. Which meant that she wasn't sorry as one by one the women went out until there was just Jane and little Lizer left. Julie stuck her head in "Jane, come and meet Sister Mary."

"Who on earth is Sister Mary? A nun or something?"

"Naw, she's the nurse wot looks after us boating families. She lives 'ere an' catches us all as we go by. She can tell you lots about us."

Jane was led on to the bank and to a small cottage, with little Lizer following behind. Ushered into Sister Mary's front parlour, she was introduced to a mature lady in full nurse's uniform. Although she was not aware of it, she was entering the presence of a legendary character.

Sister Mary Ward had become the narrow boat community's primary source of medical care for anything less than major surgery, and was to continue until well after the War, only retiring when the narrow boat community had dwindled away to a very few, and the National Health Service made access to health cover more readily available. But most importantly she was utterly trusted by the boaters; their closed community was wary of outsiders interfering with their lives (and bodies) and especially of anyone in a uniform which spoke of authority over them. In return Sister Mary was totally devoted to the boaters and their wellbeing and they knew it.

Introductions made, Julie left; little Lizer settled quietly in a corner. Jane explained briefly that she was there to see if Wrens might supplement or make up crews for narrow boats, given their shortage. Sister Mary looked thoughtful. "You have to understand that the narrow boat people are very reserved. Mostly they are families who have been on the boats for many generations and live entirely within their own community so a sudden influx of strangers would not go well with them. I suppose an odd girl or two might be acceptable on the butty but the problem is more with a shortage of men to be steerers of pairs and certainly you couldn't put an outside female into that role. If you really wanted to bring them in it would probably be better for them to make up whole crews than to add to family boats. But whether girl crews could do it, I doubt. You must have seen by now that it is physically demanding and highly skilled work. I've seen the results of all too many accidents and even deaths on the cut and untrained females would really struggle to do anything here safely."

Jane nodded. "Yes, I don't think I have ever worked harder than the last few days and wouldn't have a clue how to run a boat myself. All I am doing so far is tagging along and doing what I'm told. These people are really skilled in an understated way."

"That's because they have done it from earliest childhood. Uneducated they might be but stupid they are not and their understanding of working the cut is bred into them to be second nature. There's probably no reason why outsiders couldn't learn if the boat people were willing to teach them but they are so reserved that I wonder if they would be any good at teaching. Just to learn the job by working with them and absorbing it all would take far too long; the war would probably be over before they got sufficiently good at it to be any use and that doesn't really do anything to help the present shortages.

Jane smiled. "I'll need to think about this one; it is proving to be a lot more complicated than I had been led to expect. But thanks for your thoughts."

"You are welcome; anything I can do to help these people and life on the cut, I'm happy to do."

Jane stood up to go. As she did so a little hand slipped into hers and Lizer trotted out with her. Something had changed outside; a southbound narrow boat pair had tied up and Julie was sitting in the butty's steering well talking animatedly to a dark young man. 'Well well,' thought Jane, 'so that's what Julie's Jeb looks like.' Standing on the bank with Lizer in hand, Jane was debating what to do when Suey stuck her head out and called "Come Lizer, bedtime." The little girl looked up at Jane and asked "Will you tuck me up?"

"Yes Lizer if your mummy will let me. Come on, let's get you off to bed." Emerging from Suey's boat with duty done Jane waved to Julie and retreated to *Endymion*, wondering what might happen next.

Soon Julie joined her, looking slightly flushed. " 'Ave yew got a good dress? We loik to look a bit better in the pub an' I've got a super one."

"I'm afraid not; I didn't bring anything like that with me, so it will just have to be my working rig."

"Oh well never moind but bring yer squeeze box. That'll be good in the pub."

Finding their way into the *Boat* Inn Jane and Julie joined a group of younger people of both sexes standing by the bar. Elsewhere in the room a strict segregation seemed to be in force, with the older women all sitting together along one wall and the senior men sitting by the bar. Jane was introduced to Jeb and his friend Sam who offered her a drink. A pint seemed the best bet for not getting too drunk but she noticed that port and lemon seemed to be the drink of choice for the women apart from a few of the older ones drinking pints like herself.

"Yew do a lot of this warfarin' stuff? We 'eard about yew rescuin' boats down at Lime 'Ouse."

"Oh that. I only did what had to be done. I've been doing stuff like that for a while now."

"Is that 'ow yer face got marked?"

"Oh yes, shrapnel at Dunkirk, I'm afraid. Luckily my fiancé understands and doesn't mind."

"Yew is gettin married?"

"Yes indeed, in September war permitting."

This clear indication that she was engaged seem to ease the atmosphere and the worried glance Julie had given her when Jeb seemed quite enthusiastic about meeting Jane, eased off her face.

"'Ow d 'yew loik being on the boats?"

"Fascinating but damn hard work. I don't think I've ever worked harder than that first day heading north from the depot."

"That's nothing. Yew wait till you get to the stairway to the stars; that's the Hatton twenty-one an' that is real hard work."

"I suppose you are all used to the life but for someone like me it is serious hard work."

"yeah, we 'eard you was really stroving; not loik that navy bloke they sent. It must be good fer yew, not bein' told what to do all the time."

"Well it's all right for you, knowing what to do. I have to be told everything here."

"So you're used to bein' told what to do?"

"Not entirely boys. I go my own way as much as I can while in uniform."

"Go your own way? I bet yew've been told what to do since yew was borned. We'se all told wot to do when we'se little kids. Are you a scholard?"

"If you mean did I go to school, then yes of course. It's you people who are unusual not going to school. Have you had any schooling at all?"

"Not really. We gets the odd day in the school at the depot but never enough to learn to read 'n write."

There were half a dozen young people in Jane's group and she looked round them. "So none of you can read or write? Doesn't that bother you?"

"Not really. Yew don't miss what yew've never 'ad. We don't need it fer goin' on the canals an' we don't have nothin' else. Yew spent your child time at school?"

"That's right. I was sent away when I was eleven."

"Yous was sent away? Then wot?"

"Well after school I went sailing in the Mediterranean for six months then joined the Wrens."

"So yew went from home to school to a boat then the Wrens. Yew've spent you's 'ole life bein' told what to do. 'Ere we is free to go as we please, just 'ave to earn our money carryin' cargoes."

Jane had never thought of her life like this, seeing herself as a free person but yes, they were right weren't they?

"But the pressure to keep getting ahead and running the next cargo is relentless. How can you think of yourselves as free when you've got that as a constant?"

" 'Ow we do it is our business. It was better wen we was number ones an' was entirely free but even strovin' fer the canal company we goes our own way. Dad 'as never forgiven the company fer forcin' 'im to sell his boats to them."

"Oh, why did they do that?"

"Company wanted all the business to theyselves. So they took the contracts away from the number ones an' forced us to sell our boats to them. Dad still gets angry about it an' after this daft war is over lots of the old number ones is goin' to retire an' leave the cut. But at least we'se free to run our boats as we loik. Not loik yew, 'avin' to salute and do wat yew's told all the time."

"It's not all like that but you do have a lot of freedom within limits, I suppose."

This window into her life was interrupted by Mrs S coming over and asking Jane to play her squeeze box. A couple of the steerers had small accordions and had been trying a few simple tunes, so Jane launched into a dance number which they were able to follow. A lively hour past with singing and even a little dancing; Jane found her beer glass being topped up frequently and had to exercise a little discreet restraint. By closing time the packed little pub was in a happy uproar with everyone in high spirits and the war seeming a long way away. Making their way back to the boats Mrs S said "Call me Rose, dearie. Yew could be one of us any time."

"Well thanks,.........Rose." Jane suspected she had just been paid a high compliment but as she lay down the boys' words were haunting her. Was she really so restricted in her life? It had never seemed that way but yes, she supposed she was a natural conformist, at ease with the boundaries and petty restrictions of her life. As long as this blasted war went on she'd have to put up with them; after it, perhaps David and she could find some way to be freer. But being a Naval officer's wife was not going to give her that sort of freedom, was it? She gently drifted off trying to make sense of it all. These people might not be schooled but they were so perceptive and seemed to have their lives sorted in their own particular way. Julie, Jane noticed, was missing. 'Why am I not surprised' she thought to herself with an inward grin.

CHAPTER SIX:
First Last Lap

Despite her late night it was Julie who woke Jane in the morning. "Daylight's comin' in an' we'll be off soon."

Slightly thick of head, Jane rolled out. "Dad says will yew take the butty with Maw wile I go on the motor with 'im."

Within minutes they were on the move. Rounding the first bend, Jane to her dismay saw a tunnel mouth. "I suppose we go through that? Is it a long one?"

Rose smiled "This 'ere's Blizzerth an' yes it's the longest tunnel on the cut."

'Oh dear' thought Jane, finding the prospect of a long tunnel daunting. As the tunnel swallowed them Jane steered the butty to the right hand side and again got that feeling of being entombed, with the brickwork sliding past her just a couple of feet away. It was cold and clammy and oppressive and Jane found herself hating it. This was not helped by a quick drenching as they passed under the first of the airshafts vertically above them. Having Rose sitting on the step into the cabin was a comfort, but not much and as the tunnel went on and on Jane felt a sense of hysteria rising which she fought to keep under control. Twice they passed loaded pairs heading south and at least she was able to steer accurately and avoid hitting them. But by thirty five minutes later the north end came as a blessed relief and her sense of panic died away. It was strange, she reflected, that railway tunnels didn't bother her at all yet these canal ones were really oppressive. It had to do with their being so much more close and immediate, she thought, and being exposed to the clammy air in them made them seem much more personal. She'd never been aware of suffering from claustrophobia but then she'd never been in a tunnel like that one. "Don't you hate them?" she asked Rose, who shrugged. "It's where the canal goes so we goes too. Can't do nuffin' about that."

This fatalism was all very well but did nothing to calm Jane's sense of dislike. Back in the open air with a steady drizzle falling, they plodded on. A canal went off on the right, and a main line railway ran close to the cut for some miles but apart from that they were in deep countryside of a sort that was new to Jane. Gently rolling, agrarian and green but very pleasant, it took her mind off fretting about what the boys had said last night. This had been tugging at her mind since they started that morning; was she really that conformist? The girl who stole a boat and went to Dunkirk? But in other ways perhaps she was and they were certainly right in saying that she had always been under someone else's control throughout her life. 'When this war ends,' she thought, 'I'm going to find some way of being totally free as best I can while being a naval officer's wife.' This gently ruminative state was brought to an end by more locks looming up. "These 'ere is Bugby seven" advised Rose. "Yew can help Julie lock wheel 'em." So it was on with the heavy belt, pick up the windlass and back into what was becoming a familiar routine. At the top lock Mr S did not wait for the girls but pushed on a few hundred yards before tying up. By the time the girls got to the boats an official was going round measuring how deep in the water the boats were. The gauging rod used for this had been explained to Jane at the depot but she was surprised to see it being used again; with the official satisfied they pushed on. Soon another tunnel mouth sat in their way. 'Oh no, thought Jane, 'not another one.'

"Is this one very long?" She asked anxiously.

"Long enough. This 'ere's Branson."

So again she found herself plunged into this deeply alien world with the tunnel side sliding past just a foot or two away. "Watch for the bends in the middle," cautioned Rose. 'This is ridiculous' thought Jane as fright rose up in her. 'I really have to get a grip of myself. This is an everyday part of being on the canal and can't be so bad.' But the sense of oppressive alien creepiness persisted and she wasn't sorry to get into the drizzle again. A quarter of a mile further and they came to locks again. But these ones were going down. "That's a bit strange isn't it? The last lot went up."

"That's the way of it. Up down, up down, all the way from Lime 'Ouse to Brumagen. This 'ere is Branson. We'll stop 'ere for an hour and check on our cottage. We 'ave one just on the bank. Coom and see."

The Smythson's cottage proved to be one of a small row; they were whitewashed, low and looked ancient. Inside there were some odd bits of furniture and a big brass bed frame; despite a slight mustiness in the air it was immaculately clean. "When our Julie weds next year Mister Smythson an' me is goin' to retire ter here, an' she an' Jeb can 'ave the boats. I won't be sorry ter stop, me lumbago is troublin' me somethin 'orrible these days." Jane was a bit startled that the rock-like lady should have anything wrong with her but a life of standing alternating with heavy manual labour, all open to the weather summer and winter, was bound to take its toll. They shopped for fresh milk and vegetables and within minutes of getting back on board Mr S was wanting to go again. "Jane, yew take the motor this time." So she peeled it away from the tie-up, checked that the butty had followed on the end of the snubber and once again settled down to plodding on at a steady four miles an hour. Napton Junction came and they turned hard right to head direct to Birmingham again. Soon more locks appeared, still going down, and to Jane's surprised Mr S jumped off and worked the locks with Julie. More locks and more locks came and went, some close together, others spaced out and it was falling dark before Mr S called a halt after taking a couple of locks starting to climb again. "This 'ere's Warwick an' will do us for today."

Jane, who had been lockwheeling with Mr S for the last dozen locks while Julie drove the motor, wasn't sorry to hear that. Despite the longish peaceful stretches the horrible tunnels and multitude of locks had made it seem neverending. The smell of stew wafting from the butty had been setting her tummy rumbling for some time and for once there was enough to give her a good satisfying plateful. Again, they had stopped close by a pub, the *Cape of Good Hope,* and with their stew eaten it was time for pints all round. This one was not full of canal people as the *Boat* had been, but had a timeless scrubbed wood simplicity to it, even having sand on the floor and Jane found it comfortingly cosy.

As they settled for sleep Julie remarked, "Yew'll be fresh for Hatton in the morning. That's good 'cos yew'll need to be." Jane was too tired to care and was asleep in moments.

Up again at first light, round a bend they came to a flight of locks climbing away up a steep hill. "Now yew sees why we calls it the 'stairway to heaven'. C'mon Jane, we got work to do." By nine o'clock they reached the top lock of the twenty-one in the Hatton flight; Jane's hands had a fresh set of blisters and her whole body ached. But Mr S was pleased. "That was good goin'. I couldn't have done it faster meself. We'll make Tyseley today all right." When had Jane had a compliment like that? Yes of course, the old admiral they had taken down the Thames to Southend telling her that men could not have done any better. It was the same sort of back-handed praise, intended as commendation, which nevertheless left her thinking 'why should men be any better? I can do it and show that I can do it'. But actually she wasn't sorry that there were no more locks for a while and they had a long level pound to plod along.

They passed up the five locks of the Knowle flight in mid-afternoon and from then on the surroundings became increasingly industrialised. Jane, who by now felt pretty confident in her steering, was on her own on the motor when she took a sharp bend trying to stay in the middle of the canal as usual. But suddenly the boat heeled over dramatically, and stopped. Mr S rushed out and looked around. To Jane's surprise he laughed. "Ah, Muck Bend caught yew, eh? Maybe I should've warned yew. Come 'n see wat we do now." He took the engine out of gear, collected the long shaft and went forward on the top planks, Jane trailing in his wake. Pole on bank he pushed backwards then handed the pole to Jane, " 'ere, you try". She pushed. Nothing happened. She pushed a bit harder. Still nothing. Getting cross, she heaved with all her strength and suddenly the boat slid backwards and off the mudbank. This sudden movement back and upright again with Jane still pushing hard threw her off balance and into the canal where she made the forceful acquaintance of the mud bank. Going head first deep into the slimy mud was terrifying and for a brief moment she panicked before wrenching herself out of it and scrambling back onto the boat. Her head was encased in black glutinous and smelly mud which covered her face completely. This time she did panic. "I can't breathe, I can't see, it tastes vile," she shrieked as she clawed at her face. Mr S pulled a bucket out of the cratch and threw bucketful after bucketful of canal water at her head. This got rid of the worst of it, then a rag thrust into her hand enabled her to clear her face. Shivering, shaking with fright and cold, plastered in stinky mud and thoroughly angry with herself beneath the panic, she glared at Mr S who seemed to regard the incident with a wry amusement. "Yew has done well to stay out of the water till now. Shut yewself in the motor cabin an' have a good wash. I'll get Julie to fetch yew some new clothes."

Cleaned up as best she could with only a small basin of cold water, Jane re-emerged to find the boats were in an urban landscape with houses and factories passing by. Buses and lorries roared overhead and trams clanged over the bridges. After an hour of this Mr S said, "There's Tyseley" nodding to the left bank where three pairs of narrow boats were tied up already, a small crane dipping into one of them. Suey stood in the stern of her butty and gave them a big wave.

As soon as they were tied up, Rose took charge of Jane. "Don't worry love, we've all gone in there."

"Yes, but I bet you didn't go in head first. That was horrible."

"Come on the butty with me an' we'll get some hot water ter clean yew oop a bit better. With three boats ahead o' us we'll not get empty termmorrer so we've good time ter get yews clothes scrubbed. We'll do a big washing an' yew can help."

Her head was plunged into the basin of hot water and her hair scrubbed vigorously by strong hands. With at least her head cleaner Jane felt better but memories of the desperate feeling of being encased in the mud kept washing over her; this was as bad as the faces at Dunkirk or being trapped on the Thames with the tide rising round her. Emotionally wrung out Jane lay on the side bed while her hosts bustled round cleaning the cabin.

In the midst of this Suey came on board with Lizer in tow. " 'Ere, she wants to comfort yew."

A warm little body lay down beside Jane, snuggling up and whispering "Yew'll be all right, promise." This was an unexpected balm and she hugged the little girl tightly, drifting into semi-consciousness.

That evening there was a family move to go to the pictures so Jane offered to babysit and sitting in Suey's butty with three little children sleeping peacefully helped to soothe her shredded nerves. The journal she had been keeping was two days behind so she wrote that up, trying to avoid being too dramatic about the mud, then wrote to David. Just for the moment the war, the Navy, even her fiancé all seemed impossibly remote, almost irrelevant, and her world shrunk to a little wooden cabin and a group of family ties.

Julie had promised Jane a lie-in as they were not likely to get unloaded that day, but this translated into Jane's usual time of 0630 rather than the first light of the last few days. Both stoves were set roaring and with a tap close by giving a constant water supply, ample hot water was boiled up for the washing. Rose produced a large wooden tub and a wooden shaft with a cross-handle on one end and an open-jawed knob on the other. Jane asked, "What's this?"

Rose smiled grimly. "That's the dolly. We use it to beat and stir the clothes in the dolly tub," and here she kicked the wooden tub "An' it works very well."

A scrubbed wooden board with a mangle clamped to one end was set up on trestles on the bank. A fire was started and a large galvanised tub set on it to keep up the supply of hot water. Suey joined them with her laundry and it was plain that Jane was expected to join in, so the four women set to. Jane watched fascinated as the dolly was used to pound and swirl clothes in the tub, then those with stains were spread out and scrubbed on the wooden board. Rinsing was done in the canal, slightly to Jane's surprise, before they were put through the mangle and hung up along the length of the boats.. All this was a new world to her who had never washed more than her own smalls but the casually effective teamwork with almost no instructions but a constant stream of chatter and gossip, was impressive. Her own filthy mud-stained clothes were laid on the board and she was invited to scrub them. She could hardly say no, so set to and managed to get them less stained, at least. By lunch time the work was done and strings of clean laundry fluttered in the breeze. Rose smiled, "I allus loiks ter see a good clean wash," she confided.

With the women busy, Suey's children had played on the bank with some from the other boats but Jane had noted four that looked dirty and unkempt and did not join with the others. The boat they came from had a scruffy neglected air to it too. She asked Rose about these children. "Humph. Them's Rodneys. Don't go near 'em."

"Rodneys?"

"Yeah, wot we calls them lazy dirty boogers. Got no pride an' it shows. You'll find 'em round the cut. Don' go near 'em, they got fleas an' lice an' all sorts. But they knows to keep away from us proper boaters."

"Not like you then. Don't the steerers have something to say about the state of their boats?"

"Naw. Like takes to like. Mr Smythson took a good look at 'ow moi mother kept 'er boats before 'e suggested that we wed. If she'd been a Rodney he wouldn't 'ave gone near me."

Jane could only raise her eyebrows at this little window into another part of the canal life. In the afternoon the Smythson's cabins were given an extra polish then Rose and Julie settled down with their crochet. Jane had already noted bits of fine work about the cabins and now she saw where it came from. "Don' you do crosher Jane?"

She shook her head. "Not the sort of thing I've ever come across. I'm handy with needle and thread and good at ropework but this is new. Can you show me?"

So Rose and Julie spent the afternoon showing Jane how to do it and tentatively she tried a bit which to her surprise worked well. As ever little Lizer was by her side and paid close attention to the instructions.

Next morning Suey's pair were pulled under the crane and by late morning were empty. It was Smythson's turn then, and by mid afternoon they were also empty. Both pairs were now under orders to go by the Bottom Road to the Coventry coal-fields and had arranged to go "butty" that is, to travel together and help each other through the narrow locks they were now facing.

"Soon as missus an' Julie are back from shoppin' we'll loose an' go."

But there was a short delay when they returned; Jane had noticed Suey in old dirty clothes and now Julie disappeared into the butty to re-emerge in tattered blackened old rags of clothes. She looked at Jane in her usual white front and bell bottoms. " 'Aven't yew got any old things to wear? The next bit is terrible dirty." But all Jane could do was shake her head and hope that it wasn't as bad as they said.

It seemed no time before they were confronted with the first of the narrow locks. At first Jane found these uncomfortable, their narrow confines seeming very tight after the Grand Union's broad locks she had become used to. Going butty meant that the locks had to be turned for each boat in turn. Mr Smythson had explained "We's not allowed to stop on this section so we'll go motor, then the butties, then second motor. Each boat 'll take one wheeler with them down the length. You watch wat Julie does in the first one then yew can take our butty through."

What Jane had not expected was being handed a cotton line from their butty's masthead and told to pull. Julie showed her how to get the rope over a shoulder then wound round her waist several times. Even light the boat was a heavy pull and she had to dig in with her footing to get it to move. Through the first lock it was hard work but not too unpleasant. At the second lock it all changed. This one was filthy, with black oily slime coating the lock sides, filth and cinders and horse dung forming a rough surface on the area round the lock. Now Jane saw why the boat people hated this route so much. In no time the cotton line, reasonably white at the start, was reduced to a black sliminess of its own which rapidly reduced her clothes to a similar state of primeval filth of black stripes and smudged stains. She rapidly developed an angry resentment at having to work like a horse. Pulling the butty from lock to lock meant constant digging in, hauling with all her strength while the rope cut in to her shoulder painfully. It was head down and struggle, with the added nastiness of getting filthier with each lock. Nine locks later with the daylight fading they came to a sharp elbow bend; once poled round it Rose called to Jane, "That's all of them 'orrid ones. We'll be tyin' up soon."

"Well thank goodness. Being a horse is hard work. How you manage it all the time, I don't know." Ahead she saw the other butty and as she pulled her butty in she saw Julie and Suey equally filthy.

"There's more bowhaulin' ter come but at least the locks aren't so dirty."

Bacon and sausages from the frying pan made supper basic but filling.

Jane was so exhausted she could do little more than flop on the side bed. Suey called in with all three of her brood who distributed themselves round various laps fairly indiscriminately. This was something that Jane had noticed before, the little ones secure in a general aura of love and affection. Even Mr S smiled benignly from his perch in the hatchway. Lizer came to snuggle up to Jane but was warned, "Oh Lizer, I'm utterly filthy and you wouldn't want to get your nice clean frock covered in the muck I've got."

"All roit; maw, can I cuddle Jane?"

Suey waved an agreeable hand and Jane found her little shadow cuddled close. "Yew tired, Jane?" All Jane could do was nod.

"Never moind, tomorrow's better." There was an uncanny maturity about little Lizer at times.

Her prediction was at least half true. It had been late by the time the two girls had cleaned up, scrubbing each other's backs and more inaccessible bits and sharing several kettles of hot water. Jane was struck by the way Julie treated this as natural; There was nothing intimate about it, feeling more like an extension of the enveloping family closeness which she was evidently being pulled into. And that felt good, which was more than could be said for taking the Bottom Road.

First light came all too soon and groaning Jane turned out for another day of locks and bowhauling. At least these locks were cleaner. Along this canal they were meeting many boats going the other way, and almost all of them were single unpowered boats being towed by a horse. Their steersmen would pass with a gruff "'Ow do" but as on the Grand Union the wives were elaborately polite to each other as they passed. "Good day to you, Mrs Smythson, 'tis a fine day."

" 'Tis too. Good day to you, Mrs Jackson." They all seemed to know each other.

Having cleared industrial Birmingham they were soon in flatter countryside which allowed a steady Easterly wind to blow the boats about and make bowhauling harder work than it need be. Somewhere along the way the locks changed from downhill to going up, and the day's work ended at the top of a long flight. Again Jane was utterly exhausted but at least this time she had more or less stayed clean, which made a pleasant change. "We'll get loaded tomorrow" promised Mr S by way of encouraging Jane. All she could think was, 'Oh no, more work'.

CHAPTER SEVEN:
Changing Places

They cast off with the dawn creeping in, passed Suey's pair where her family were still asleep and reached the Bedworth loading arm by mid morning. A nearly full pair was just finishing so it looked promising that the Smythsons would also be loaded that day. The cargo was boiler coal, evenly graded lumps easier to work with than the mixed size household coal which was the other mainstay of southbound cargoes. They were called in to load in early afternoon, the coal dropping down a chute direct from railway wagons. Here it was Mr S's turn to emerge in old and stained clothing, while Rose and Julie went round closing the cabins as tightly as they could. "Coal dust gets everywhere" explained Julie to Jane's enquiring gaze. Under close supervision from Mr Smythson the coal was loaded to get the boats trimmed just a couple of inches by the stern, Julie and Jane being called at regular intervals to pull each boat in turn along the wharfside to keep empty hold under the loading spout. Jane rapidly felt what they meant about coal dust. It got up her nose, had a harsh taste and rapidly clogged up her hair.

Memories of coaling the picket boat at Dover came back, with the same all-pervasive dust and grit. At least she wouldn't be trying to smarten up for a date at the end of this process.

The whole loading took about three hours then they pulled back to let Suey's pair in. "No need to sheet up with coal," explained Rose when Jane queried what still had to be done. As soon as they were ready Mr S was calling for them to loose off. "We should make Sutton Stop tonight," he called across to Suey, "See you there." Once again the boats were deep loaded with just a few inches of freeboard which looked seriously perilous to Jane but they had made the run north like that without any problems so she just had to assume southbound would be the same.

As soon as they were on the move Rose and Julie fell to a frenzy of cleaning, leaving Jane to steer the butty. Both cabins were thrown open and Jane saw why they were being so particular. There was indeed a film of coal dust over everything in the cabins and being greasy, sticky stuff it had to be wiped off.

As soon as Rose had finished the motor's cabin she took the elum from Mr S and he got busy with the mop over the cabin roof, finishing with spinning the mop in his hands to dry it as all the steerers did. Jane had been intrigued by this spinning before and made a mental note to learn how.

For the first twenty minutes after leaving they made good progress; then there was a loud grunt from the stern, a bang from the engine and it fell silent. Julie looked out from the butty cabin. "Put us on the bank," she instructed. So trying to judge it as best she could Jane came up close behind the motor and stemmed the bank, stopping the boat.

Mr S disappeared into the engine room and emerged a short while later looking very gloomy. "Looks like we picked up somethin' big on the blades," he reported, "And that's broken the coupling and casing on the back of the engine. Nuffin I can do about it, we'll 'ave ter get help."

He was still standing around looking gloomy when Suey's boats arrived. "Our engine's broke," he called. We're for the yard now."

"Want a tow to Sutton Stop?" Suey's Bill called over.

"Yeah, that'd be good."

It took a short while to sort out tow lines and get everything connected up but once again Jane could see the skill these families brought to the job. Getting on the move was a slow process but as the lead motor's propeller took hold of the load they managed to creep along and pulled in to Hawksbury Junction just before dark, watched by the many boatmen whose boats were tied up at Sutton Stop. Safely tied up, the family retired for a supper of tripe and onions; this was a new experience for Jane whose first instinct was to recoil from it but then she thought 'What the hell, if they can manage it so can I' and surprised herself by finding it quite acceptable.

Supper over, Mr Smythson looked at Jane, "Oi think we may be 'ere for a woile. That engine's dead an' we'll 'ave to get a new one. Wot do yew want ter do?"

"Well, I've still got a week before I have to report back to headquarters. There's probably not a lot of point in just sitting here, nice though it is to be with you. Is there anything else I could do?"

"Oi don' know but we'll go to the *Greyhound* this evening an' see wat's doin'. An' termorrer Oi'll interdooce yew ter Mr Veater 'cos he will know all wat's goin' on."

"The Greyhound?"

"Yeah, the pub across the basin." He pointed it out.

"That's your local when you get here? It will be popular with the boating people?"

"We all go there. We'll 'ear wat's wat."

The constant exposure to dust, grease and dirt was making Jane's hair feel like straw. Another scrub and shampoo was now needed to get rid of the coal dust but left the hair even rougher.

Julie's Jeb was not around so they had to wait until Mr Smythson was ready before they could go into the pub. "Women aren't allowed in on their own," explained Julie and again Jane had this feeling of stepping backwards into a previous age. As at the *Boat*, Jane found women sitting on one side with men on the other apart from a mixed group of young adults clustered round the bar. Jane sensed that this group were being watched closely by the elders who presumably were their parents.

Julie made introductions and the men clustered round. Jane felt like a giraffe among these short stocky men; the girls had an equally muscular air about them. They were gossiping about happenings along the cut until one of the boys turned to Jane " I 'eard yew took a look into the canal mud. 'Ow yew enjoyin' life on a narrow boat?"

"That mud was horrible and I hated it. As for the life, it's different that's for sure. I'm finding it fascinating but my goodness you guys work hard and the living conditions are tough. "

"Wen this war's over maybe things will be better. A good socialist government will see us roit, with decent pay an' better boats. Schoolin' for the kiddies an' no more sending us by the bottom road."

Jane grimaced. "You have all my sympathies about the bottom road. At least a post-war government could clean it up. It doesn't have to be that filthy. But the boats are owned by commercial companies so surely the government won't make any difference to them?"

"A proper socialist government would take us over, canals, boats an' everything. Then things'd get better. "

Mr Smythson had been passing by with a fresh pint and overheard this. "Yew just stop yer socialist nonsense, young Hall, it's bein' independent wat makes our lives worth it."

"Yeah, and allus hard oop, strovin' away fer tuppence. A decent standard of life'd be a good trade for your precious independence Mr Smythson. An' look wat yours got yew. Yew was a good number one till the canal company took yer contract from under yew and yew 'ad no choice but sell yer boats to them 'an go to work for them."

This debate went on for some time then Julie, clearly fed up with it, demanded "Jane, play us a toon." With some assistance from a couple of boatmen with melodeons, she had them singing happily.

As closing time was drawing near Jane noticed Rose and her captain in deep discussion, then she was called over to join them. "Jane, 'ere's an idea fer yew. I've been talking with Nellie 'Arbutt an' she's got a problem. Her captain's been taken into 'ospital with a bad stomach an' it may be weeks before 'e gets out. They 'as their own horse boat loaded with coal for Lechlade an' she only 'as her little runnerboat with her on the boat so she can't get ahead. 'Ow about yew go with her an 'elp her down the Hoxford Canal? That'd let her get ahead an' give yew somethin' to do instead o' sittin' 'ere with us."

"Well, that is an interesting idea. You wouldn't be offended if I went on another boat?"

"Lor' bless me no, Jane. Yew was sent to learn an' yew won't learn much sittin' here at Sutton. An' yew would be doing Nellie a big favour. I've told her 'ow good yew are."

"Well thanks, I suspect it's a very superficial goodness but maybe I can help a bit."

"Oi think so. Come 'an meet Nellie."

Jane had been expecting another venerable lady like Rose so was surprised to be introduced to a younger woman. It was difficult to judge the ages of canal boat women with their deeply weathered and toil- lined faces but this slim woman was probably no more than forty, guessed Jane. The deal was done quickly, with Nellie Harbutt very pleased to see a way to get ahead when she had been facing weeks of forced inactivity. They agreed to go to see Mr Veater in the morning.

Ernest James Veater – universally known simply as Mr Veater by the narrow boat community – was a dominant figure in their lives. He worked from a little wooden shack control office at Hawksbury, the junction known as Sutton Stop by the Narrow boat people. With the able assistance of the indomitable Miss Edwards, Mr Veater allocated cargoes and boats for their next turn. This gave him a powerful position in itself but he did much more, concerning himself with the boaters' health and welfare and knowing every steersman, his family and their abilities. After years of working for first the Oxford then the Grand Union Canal Companies, by 1941 he had become a government employee developing the wartime boat allocation scheme which was still in its early days. Applied equally to all the boat owners' craft, it turned into a highly efficient way of employing the boats and keeping cargo flowing. In a benign way his word was law among the boaters.

Jane had heard about Mr Veater and had intended to ask his opinion about the use of Wrens on narrow boats anyway but now there was a double reason to see him. Early next morning she made her way round the basin to Nellie Harbutt's boat, the *Fidelity,* and knocked on the cabin side in approved fashion. Brightly painted along the cabin side was *HENRY HARBUTT INDEPENDENT CARRIER, REG. BANBURY NO. 59.* The panels with Roses and Castles shone in the morning light and the whole boat was immaculate. Nellie looked out of the cabin, smiled and invited Jane on board. A young girl was sitting in the cabin's corner "Jane, this is my runnerboat, Ginny. She's my sister Ellie's girl an' 'as coom ter me ter help. She's real good at the job."

"Hello Ginny. How old are you?"

"Please miss, I'm ten." Ginny was shy but carried a self-confidence which spoke of being usefully at home here with her aunt.

Jane turned to Nellie. "Assuming we sort things out with Mr Veater, when do you want to get going?"

"First thing termmorrer morning. I'll need ter get some food an' fill up the water cans but then we can go."

"That's fine. If I give you five pounds will that be enough for my keep?"

"Yeah, that's plenty. Got any coupons?"

"I'll have to see how much is left in the emergency ration book I gave to Mrs Smythson. I handed it over when I joined."

"Yew any good at cookin'?"

"No, I'm afraid not. It's something I've never done. Will that be a problem?"

"Naw; you might need ter peel the spuds or stir the pot sometimes but Ginny's good at it an' I do most of it onywiy. Jane smiled at Ginny. "What do you do on the boat?"

Ginny was clearly puzzled by the question. "Please miss, I do everythin'."

"You mean work the locks and things like that?"

"Oh yes, an' steer an' work the hanimal an' clean the boat an I'm gettin' good at socks."

"Socks?"

Nellie butted in. "She means knitting socks. She's gettin' really neat at turning a heel now."

'Now there's a skill I haven't got' thought Jane. Again she turned to Nellie. "Will we all be living in the cabin here?"

"Yeah, Ginny can share the bed 'ole with me wile yew are on board an' yew can 'ave the side bed."

A knock on the cabin side drew them up on deck to find Mr Smythson waiting. "Come with me an' I'll interdoos yew to Mr Veater."

There were several steerers waiting by the control office door, so the trio joined the queue and waited while the men ahead of them got their orders, loading coal from one or other of the collieries in the Coventry coalfield. The trio's turn came and Mr Veater gave Jane an appraising look. But Mr Smythson stepped in. " 'Ow do, Mr Veater. This is Jane Beacon wat 'as come from the Navy ter see wat we're about. An' Nellie wants a word with yew too."

"Ah yes, I've been told about you Miss Beacon. How are you getting on?"

"It's quite fascinating, Mr Veater. We were doing well until yesterday when *Rome's* engine blew up. It looks like we're stuck here for some time now."

"So I understand. The engine is a write-off, Jake?"

"Oi think so. The casing's gone at the back of the engine and somethin' 'orrible 'as got round the blades. It's a new engine an' drydock for us I reckon. Probably need a tow down to Branson. But the mechanics are comin' today an' we'll see what they 'ave ter say."

Mr Veater turned to Nellie. "Mrs Harbutt, what did you want to see me about?"

"Well, it's like this Mr Veater. Yew know my 'Enery is in the 'ospital an' may stay for a while? So we was kind of stuck. But Jane 'ere is hofferin' to come with me down to Hoxford. With little Ginny I reckon the three of us can manage so we're thinkin' of goin' in the mornin'. Is that all right with yew?"

"So long as you're happy with that, I don't see why not. The message from the cut is that Miss Beacon has been doing very well and will make a useful mate for you. I'll let them know down the line that you are coming. Have you any news of when Henry may come out of hospital?"

"Afraid not. They's still tryin' ter work out what's the matter with 'im'. His stomach is troublin' 'im somethin' terrible. Fer now we just 'ave ter wait an' see."

Mr Veater Turned to Jane. "Are you happy with this arrangement, Miss Beacon?"

"Yes I think so. There's not a lot of point in my sitting here for a week and it will be very educational to go on a horseboat. I gather it's a quite different way of going."

"It is all of that. I have to let your office know what you're doing so I will let them know that you will be going to Oxford instead of returning to London. Should take four, maybe five days to Oxford then there's the time up the Thames to Lechlade; say another two or three days. That would be a good use of your last week on the cut. I gather you'd like to speak to me about the whole business of why you are here?"

"That's right, my understanding is that you make a lot of the decisions and know the boat people intimately. So you'd be a sensible person to get an opinion from."

Mr Veater turned to the other two. "Would you mind leaving us to it? I'll see you later."

On their own, Mr Veater motioned to Jane to sit down. "You start," he suggested.

"Well, you know the background story, I think?" He nodded.

"I must say these last few weeks have been an utterly fascinating eye-opener into a new world for me. These people are hard-working and tough in a way that is lost nowadays in most of England. That and the overwhelming sense of family are my dominant impressions, which makes me doubtful about trying just to add odd Wrens to existing family units. They are a kind-hearted and friendly lot but are so committed to working and getting ahead that adding Wrens would only work if they were willing to work as hard and adapt to the boaters' way of living. I can see a lot of girls being unimpressed by a bucket in the engine room for a toilet and no matter how hard you try, one is always dirty. And I really don't think any kind of militarised arrangement would work with the boaters. They are such free spirits that inserting a uniformed element into their way of life just wouldn't work."

Mr Veater smiled. "I am pleased that your people have sent someone willing to see and learn, not just retreat behind their existing prejudices. You are right in what you say, but does that mean that women off the bank would not be suitable at all?"

Jane considered this. "I hadn't thought of it that way. I suppose there's no reason why all girl crews off the bank shouldn't drive a boat but they'd need to be awfully strong and determined to survive the demands of the job. Now you mention it, that's a good idea; I have to write a report when I get back to base and I'll suggest 'not Wrens, but civvy women might do'. Are you seriously short of crews?"

"The GUCC is, partly because the boss is a bit dictatorial and boaters don't like that sort of attitude. I think we'll probably mull this one over a bit more but who knows, something may come of it eventually. Now, is there anything else you want to discuss just now?"

"Yes, one more thing. Why do you send the boats round by the Bottom Road? It's a horrible route and causes more discontent than anything else. You really shouldn't do it."

"The problem is that it has plenty of water where going round by Braunston always threatens a bit of a shortage. If the pressure eases off a bit we'll look at letting the steerers decide for themselves, which way to go."

"They'll all go south, I can tell you."

Mr Veater smiled gently. "No doubt. Now if that's everything I really must get on."

"That's my lot for now. I'll get a copy of my report sent to you when I write it."

Dismissed, Jane strolled back to the Smythson boats, greeting various boaters she had met in the pub the previous evening. It felt good that they all gave her a friendly greeting back.

Back on *Endymion* she packed her gear into the trusty kitbag, helped by little Lizer who had popped up as soon as Jane arrived back on board.

"Are yew goin' away?"

"Yes Lizer, I'm going on that other boat across the basin. I know you'll be moving again tomorrow but this boat isn't, so I have to do something else."

"That's sad. I like yew, Jane."

"I know Lizer and I like you too but you know how it is; your boats have to keep moving."

"Can I 'ave yer 'at for a present?"

"You what? Yes, I suppose so. It's probably a bit big for you but yes, you can have it. Ask your mother to tighten it a bit at the back."

That Wren's hat did little Lizer for years, a testimony to the soundness of the Navy's basic specifications.

The pub that night proved to be a rowdy and lively place, with Jane finding herself drawn ever deeper into acceptance by the boating community.

Farewells to the Smythsons proved difficult, with even Mr Smythson unbending enough to say "Not bad for someone off the bank" and Julie positively tearful.

"Can I write to you, Julie?"

"Jane, I can't read nor write. 'Ow am I goin' ter read it?"

"Ask someone to read it for you, I suppose. Doesn't it bother you, not being able to read or write?"

"Not mostly. I suppose yew don's miss wat yew've never 'ad." But it'd be nice to read a letter from yew."

"I'll send you one anyway to practise on."

And with final farewells said, Jane moved over to *Fidelity.*

CHAPTER EIGHT:
Horse Power

As on the Smythsons' boats, Jane found herself awoken at daylight by the others on the move and found the kettle singing nicely. "I'll just get the hanimal then we'll be off." With that Nellie went onto the bank and disappeared. Ginny asked "Do you drink tea?" And set about making a large potfull. By the time tea was drunk Nellie was back "Right, Hanimal is round the corner ready for us. Jane, can yew bowhaul?"

"Oh yes I can bowhaul but why not get the horse to do it?"

" 'Cos we've got to get round the corner first. We'll attach him in the stop lock." So Jane, still half asleep, found herself on the towrope cotton line again. This was getting to be a bit of a tedious procedure. *The turn into the Oxford Canal from Sutton Stop basin is notorious: An acute angled hairpin bend under a roving bridge, it has made hard work for boaters ever since its creation in the mid-1800s.* The boat was pulled down until half its length was past the corner, then Jane was instructed to pull round while Nellie shafted the stern. Half an hour of heavy pulling and pushing got them round and into the stop lock. A large mule was waiting patiently by the lock; with only a foot of rise the stop lock was no obstacle and Jane watched with interest as the mule was hitched up and Ginny led it away until the weight came on the line. The mule felt the load come on and leant into it, applying gentle steady pressure to get the boat on the move. "Once he gets goin' Billy will plod on all day," remarked Nellie.

"Billy?" Queried Jane.

"The hanimal. We've 'ad 'im about five years now an' he's a good 'un. Hard worker but nice 'n friendly. Do you know about these hanimals?"

"I'm afraid not; for me it was always boats."

"Oh well, yew'll learn a bit if you loik."

There was something different about their progress after being on the Smythson pair, and at first Jane couldn't put a finger on it. Then it dawned: no engine noise. The single cylinder Bolinder that had chugged away in *Rome* had not been particularly dominant but its sound was always there, even reaching the butty. Now, apart from the faintest of hoof sounds, they were moving in silence. This meant that Jane found herself much more conscious of the world around her. Progress on a horseboat came with a sense of restfulness after the constant need to push on which had imbued life on the motor pair with such urgency. Settled down, Nellie said "'Ere, you take the elum and I'll get some breakfast." She hovered round Jane for the first five minutes while Jane adapted to this new way of going, then disappeared into the cabin. Soon an evocative smell of frying bacon was reminding Jane of something else, some other time. What could it be? Yes of course, the time they were stuck in fog in the river of Cuckmere Haven on *Amaryllis*. How long ago that seemed, yet the smell brought the memory back sharply. The world Jane was now in was so different that it was hard to believe the two experiences belonged to the same country. Steering proved easy once she got the hang of it, finding that she had to counter a slight pull towards the bank coming from the tow line. 'Just like a little weather helm, I suppose' she thought. Nellie put her head out of the cabin and called "Ginny, breakfast." The girl waved a hand then loosened a boot that was hanging from the towrope just behind the mule. It dropped down and bounced along the ground making footstep noises, and Ginny came back as they approached a bridge hole. Two large bacon sandwiches were passed across and she trotted on ahead to catch up with Billy again. "Do you need someone at his head all the time?" queried Jane.

"Well, it's better to. 'E knows the wiy so well 'e could probably be left to get on with it, but 'e would be stopping an' starting at each juicy clump o' grass if 'e was let. The boot makes 'im think there's someone just behind 'im. 'E's a good hanimal but not terrible clever. Some people drive their hanimals from behind but oi finds Billy works better with a bit o' company so we walks beside 'is 'ead all the time. You'll soon get the hang o' that."

"Oh, I'll be doing it too?"

"Well I expect so. Poor Ginny's a good girl but she can't walk all the wiy to Hoxford."

"I'd better get some lessons first, then. Is there much to do?"

"Not really. Just keep 'im goin' and talk to 'im a little. 'E likes hearin' someone talkin' to 'im."

With the mass of Longford power station dropping behind them the canal took on a more rural air; here the cut ran across the grain of the land, instead of hugging it, with alternate cuttings and embankments. The main line railway ran alongside for a while but even the periodic thunder of a train hustling by did not disturb the greater sense of tranquillity which Jane found very pleasant as she adjusted to it. It struck her that the mule, simply plodding along, was actually making good progress and Jane remarked on this to Nellie, who grinned in reply. "Yes, all these moty people think they're real smart pushin' on but our Billy will get us there just as quick. Yew'd be surprised." In late morning the mouth of a tunnel appeared in front of them. 'Oh no, not another one' thought Jane. "Is this another of these horrid long tunnels?"

"Naw, it's only a few 'undred yards an' it's got a towpath through it so no need to go messin' about leggin' or anything."

"Thank goodness for that. I'm rapidly acquiring a hatred of canal tunnels."

Nellie looked surprised. "But they's just part o' the cut. We go where they go."

"Doesn't stop me hating them. Will there be many more?"

"Not on this run there isn't. Hoxford cut just runs round the hills."

Billy was obviously used to it and as a towpath went through the brief tunnel, he simply plodded on without hesitation or stress, rather to Jane's relief. After that the cut wiggled a bit more but progress remained good and early afternoon they came round a sharp bend to reach a staircase of three locks. The Hillmorton three were an unusual set , consisting of pairs of narrow locks side by side allowing motor and butty to pass through at the same time. But today there was something wrong. One of the locks had a motor boat in it waiting to go up, the other had a motor and a butty jammed together in the entrance. Between them two steerers were facing up to each other, shouting, swearing ferociously and waving their arms about. Nellie rolled her eyes heavenward. She shouted "Stop" to Ginny but the canal girl, already wise in such matters, had stopped the mule. Nellie guided Jane to stem the boat on the bank and wait. By now the two steerers were punching and wrestling each other, screaming abuse all the while. This was new to Jane but the way Nellie and Ginny took it calmly showed it was a normal part of life to them. "This may take a little wile" said Nellie. "We'll give the Hanimal his nostern an' 'ave some food ourselves."

"Nostern?" Queried Jane.

"Yeah, what the hanimal feeds from. " And a large round can with straps on it was produced, filled with some oats, and attached to Billy's harness as a nose bag. A tin of bully beef was opened and shared out with bread and more tea to go with it. While the three girls (and the mule) were peacefully eating, the two steerers continued their battle with more shouting than hitting but with neither showing any sign of backing down. "Oh dear," groaned Ginny "this could go on for a long time."

"But surely we could try to get them to calm down and get on with the job?" By now another pair had stemmed the bank behind *Fidelity*. Nellie shook her head. "Naw. We don' want to get involved. They'll sort it out eventually and be friends again in the pub this evenin'. It's not good for a woman to stick her nose into it when the men start this nonsense. If they're angry enough they'll hit anything an' it's bad enough strugglin' with other women without trying' the men too."

"Do the women do things like this?"

Nellie smiled, a bleak grimace that spoke volumes. "Sometimes yeah, if we're arguin' about who's first in a lock."

'I could do with Punch here' thought Jane. 'She'd sort them out'.

"Well I don't think this is good enough and I'm going to tell them so."

She hopped over onto the bank and marched up to the two struggling men. Close to, the noise was even more impressive with both suggesting that their parentage was a bit dubious. Jane stopped just out of reach. "Will you two gentlemen kindly stop this nonsense and get on with the job. There's a queue building up behind you and we all want to get ahead."

The shorter one spun round, gave Jane an enormous backhanded smack across the face which sent her spinning and snarled, "Fuck off, yew interferin' cow."

Jane picked herself up. The red mist was rising as it hadn't for a long time; they were not getting away with this. She shoved her damaged face two inches from the startled steerer's and snarled "How dare you hit me like that. Stop this now."

This coming to them in Jane's well modulated vowels startled them to stop and look at her. " 'Oo the 'ell are yew?"

"I'm the Navy girl who's been sent to see what you guys are about. And I am not impressed."

"Yew's the Navy girl wot's been sent 'ere?"

"That's right. Now sort this nonsense out. Who got here first?"

"I did an' Jackie Buttley's not stealin' my lock."

Jane recognised their faces from the pub but didn't know names. She turned "Right, Jackie, what d'you say to that?"

Jackie just growled, muttered under his breath and went back to his motor boat, backing out and letting the other steerer's butty in. Jane, conscious that she was sounding very head girl, shouted "Right, let's get on with it." She marched back her own boat nursing her face which was starting to hurt a lot, getting a friendly wave from the steerer in the pair behind *Fidelity*. Nellie looked at her and shook her head slowly. "Yew've got some guts, yew 'ave. Oi wouldn't 'ave dared do that."

"Pah. Typical men, all noise and bluster. I've dealt with worse than that, believe me. Let's hope they get on with it now."

After this little drama the boats went through speedily. The girls' turn came soon enough and they worked up the three-lock staircase, Ginny impressing Jane with her wiry strength in dealing with paddles and gates. "We'll still make Branson this evenin'," Nellie remarked. "There's good stablin' there."

"Oh, you stable Billy every night?"

"Too roit. He's our bread an' butter. We's got ter look after 'im."

Coming to clear the top lock, Nellie said "Come with me an' I'll show yew wot we 'as to do, walking the hanimal."

Billy, released from the tow rope at the bottom of the flight, had ambled up on his own and was now waiting patiently outside the top lock. The tow line was hitched to Billy's harness and he walked ahead till the load came on. Then, without instruction, He got a good footing and lent against his collar pushing hard to get the boat on the move. As it gathered way he relaxed and settled to moving ahead; once more they were progressing along the North Oxford canal. Jane noticed Ginny now on the elum and totally at ease.

"Roit. Just movin' ahead we only have ter stay by 'is 'ead an' chat to 'im. If we meets another 'orse boat we slows down an' lets the tow line go slack. The hempty boat flips its towline hover the loaded boat. Jus' watch an' yew will see us doin' it. See the wip 'ere?" And Nellie held up a thin coil which Jane had not recognised. "We cracks it to tell people we's comin'." And Nellie gave an impressive display of cracking the whip. "Can yew do that?"

"Well I've never tried. Let's see." And as they walked along Jane got a half hour tutorial in the art of cracking the whip. At first she could not get any sound out of it but it came slowly and although she was never going to be the expert that Nellie was, she could at least make it crack. "Do you ever use it on Billy?" She queried.

" 'Eavens no. We need 'im to be helpful an' whippin' 'im would do no good. Moi 'Enerey tried to once and the hanimal just stopped dead. Wouldn't budge and stood there for 'alf an 'our. That taught 'imself a lesson."

Jane laughed. "D'you know, I think I've got a lot in common with your Billy. I too refused to go after a thrashing."

"Yew got a thrashing? Oi didn't think the loiks of yew got things like that."

"Yes well, the Navy can be a bit primitive at times. I've still got the scars to prove it." Nellie looked at Jane with a new sense of respect.

A mile further on and Nellie casually said "Yew all roit if oi leave yew to it? No more locks today."

"I suppose so. What do I do if he gets difficult?"

" 'E won't. Just talk to him an' he'll pull away all day."

Left on her own Jane found the process very soothing. They were in quiet rolling countryside with only occasional signs of human activity and sparse traffic on the cut, all of it motor boats which gave *Fidelity* good space. Quietly crooning to the mule, she tried to think seriously about her situation and her world outside the immediate, and instead found herself having light random thoughts. Her own other Wren world seemed unreal, irrelevant now to her immediate world of keeping the mule happy to move the boat along the cut. In an almost trance-like condition she was startled to have Ginny suddenly appear beside her. "We'll be stoppin' in a few minutes. Auntie says will yew help tie up?" So Jane left Billy in Ginny's capable young hands and waited, hopping onto the boat at the next bridge hole. They tied up just short of the next bridge; boat secured Nellie went ashore and helped Ginny unhitch the mule. We'll take 'im to the stables now. "Yew want o coom?"

"I'll be interested to see what you do."

Nellie chatted as they went over the bridge and past the buildings lining the canal bank. "This 'ere is Branson. Lots of people doin' things fer the boats an' their crews." They passed a substantial boatyard with a lot of work going on. "That's Nurser's yard. 'E does a lot for the boaters an' his roses are lovely." It took Jane a minute to realise that Nellie meant the painted roses adorning the boat cabins. Arriving at the stables, Nellie took off Billy's harness, the crocheted ear protectors he wore to keep off the flies, topped up his feed with a full crib of hay and filled a bucket with water for him. She then gave him a rub down, checked his hooves, and combed his tail. "Roit, we can leave 'im now. 'E'll be fine till the mornin'. Let's go an' 'ave our food."

Tonight it was sausages in a stew, tastier than some of the wartime sausages of dubious content. As they ate, Jane asked "Is there much of that sort of violence goes on? I was rather appalled by it."

Nellie thought before answering. "There's allus soom around. Yew was real brave gettin' stuck in to 'em the wiy yew did. Some of 'em can be real nasty if they gets goin'. Almost allus it's over oo's first in the lock. We've all got to get ahead an' waitin' 'alf an 'our fer a turn is lost time. So we's always pushin'. But they'll be friends again in the pub this hevenin'. Us canal women don't get hit by other men; only our own man can do that. But soomtimes there's a bit of the old fisticoofs 'mongst the women too, fer the same reasons."

This intriguing answer asked half a dozen questions in Jane's mind. "You said only your own man can hit you – is there much of that?"

"It depends. Some of Rodneys, the men is allus thumpin' their miserable women. Us real boaters with some pride don't do much of it. Our men need us an' they know that they're not goin' to 'ave a nice life if they're allus beatin' up on their wives. My 'Enerey's tried it a couple of times in the past but I gave 'im such a talkin' to that he hasn't dared do it again."

"I didn't see any of that with the Smythsons – they seemed so peaceable. Was that deceptive?"

"In a wiy, yes. Rose Smythson's that hard 'er man wouldn't dare hit her. She gave one woman such a doin' over that she ended up in 'opsital. Yew wouldn't want to pick a foit with 'er."

"Well I never. Was she on her best behaviour when I was with her?"

"Not really. There's no-one on the cut would challenge her onywiy so she 'as a peaceful loif. An' yew seem to have pleased her so she was 'appy to 'ave yew on the boat."

Jane turned to Ginny. "Do the children get hit at all?"

Ginny shrugged. " A bit by their mums. Children is women's business an' the men mostly ignore us unless we do somethin' stupid; then it's a clip round the ear. My mum's tanned my bum a few times but I was up to mischief onywiy so I didn't moind. The Rodney kids have allus got black eyes an' funny bruises. It's good to 'ave a family wat's a bit strict in its ways, nicer and safer in the end." Jane had been struck by the wisdom of little Lizer and here it was again, a kid with an uncanny maturity and clarity of view.

She turned back to Nellie. "The men seem to be very much the bosses round the cut. Don't you mind?"

Nellie snorted. "Huh, they thinks they is but that's just the wiy they was brung up. It's allus the women wat keeps the show together. So far as I could see the wiy they behave is just a wiy to do as little work as possible. You'll see 'em strutting around actin' superior wile we is scrubbing our boats. But that's 'ow we was taught an' I suppose we need 'em somewhere. Moi 'Enerey's quite good by men's standards an' if he troys to get too superior I just gives 'im a piece of moi mind an' he shuts up fer a bit. Oi'm 'is bestmate and we's acterly quoit fond o' each other."

"Oh, so there's love there too?"

"O yeah, we all starts out lovey-dovey an' 'ow it goes depends on 'ow well we work together. I knew my 'Enerey was a daycent fella an' we knew from early on we'd suit each other."

Jane was fascinated. In a way this was just as life was everywhere, but somehow these people being working families gave it all an edge missing from the sedate lives of people on the bank. She smiled wryly to herself, thinking how much of the canal people's parlance she had picked up in a few weeks.

CHAPTER NINE:
On Taking A Look

Rising at dawn was starting to be natural to Jane but even so Nellie was up and gone and Ginny was stoking the range. "We'll be goin' as soon as Billy's hitched," was her brief way of saying 'good morning'. And true to that, the boat was on the move by full daylight, Ginny leading the mule and Nellie at the elum. Twenty minutes into the trip they came to a large canal junction with a small triangular island in the middle. "This 'ere's the main line fer the next five miles. Lots o' traffic so we needs to keep sharp." In no time they were being overtaken by motor pairs and keeping close to the inside for motor and horse boats passing the other way. "Yew'll know this bit."

"Will I?"

"Yeah. Yew was down this with Smythsons, goin' to Brumagen. This five mile piece is just about the busiest bit o' the cut with lots o' traffic goin' both ways. I'll be glad wen we gets past Wigram's Turn an' gets away from this lot."

Jane looked around. It was perhaps a little familiar but she wouldn't have recognised it without prompting. The steady stream of traffic was a reminder of just how busy the canal system was, but with Ginny leading the mule and cracking her whip with admirable effectiveness and Nellie steering Jane was free to take in her surroundings and the narrow boats passing in both directions. They had to pause at Napton to let boats clear before they could go straight ahead across the Grand Union entrance towards Birmingham but once beyond, Nellie relaxed visibly. "Yew will be foin now ter steer. The bottom's nearer the top along the South Hoxford so keep in the middle unless yew has to pull in fer passin' boats. Oi'll get breakfast."

Although it was still only seven o'clock, the idea of bacon butties was very attractive. 'As bad as being on the four to eight watch' thought Jane, 'except that we'll be at this all day without a break'. Her admiration of these canal people's stamina continued to grow. Nellie gave Jane her bacon butties, then stepped off the boat at a bridge hole carrying her own, took over at Billy's head and Ginny popped on board at the next bridge hole narrows. She disappeared into the cabin leaving Jane in solitude. Having passed Napton Junction the canal had gone very quiet and in the fresh morning air Jane was able to take in the remote beauty of the Cotswold countryside they were now in. This gentle reverie was interrupted as they came round a sharp right-hand bend to see, through a bridge, a flight of locks climbing up the hillside. Jane called down, "Ginny, locks coming up."

Ginny looked out, "All roit, yew go an' work the locks. Oi'll take the elum."

Jane was not entirely happy about getting orders from a ten-year-old but decided that it wasn't worth making a fuss about. The Napton flight passed easily enough with no other boats around. At the top Nellie said "Roit, yew's turn ter go with Billy. There's two more locks to come then we 'ave a nice long level pound round the countryside. Oi 'ope yew henjoy it."

And enjoy it Jane did. The glorious high summer greenery rolled away to the horizon, bird life chirped and sang in profusion, ducks and swans paddled along ahead of the boat and Billy seemed entirely at peace tramping along with Jane's casual running commentary to keep him company. The last two locks passed quickly enough, Nellie disappeared into the cabin leaving Ginny sitting on the cabin roof steering with a foot and Jane walked along with Billy for company. He seemed to be an agreeable companion, twitching an ear to say yes and giving a little shake of his head to say no as Jane regaled him with tales of launches in gales. 'Did I really get educated to Oxford entry level just to end up talking to a mule?' she mused. But somehow it was all of a piece with the rural tranquillity and sense of unreality (or was this the true reality?) around her. Somewhere out there men were fighting for their lives, bombs were being dropped and ships were shelling each other but here on the South Oxford canal it all seemed a million miles away and after the frenetic start to her career in the Wrens, Jane found this remote timeless scene a wonderful balm for her heightened emotions. One thing for sure, she reflected, doing her bit for the war effort was taking her along some very strange paths and Wren headquarters could have had no idea what they were sending her to, trying out working on a narrow boat. Her orders were to report on whether Wrens could substitute as crew. The wildly mixed experiences of the past few weeks were going to mean that her report was at best, equivocal. She had lost all sense of time, peacefully strolling along with Billy, when Nellie suddenly arrived beside her. "Toim for yew to 'ave a break. Oi'll take Billy for a stretch." Back on board, Jane found Ginny perfectly happy to go on steering so she lay on the fore end of the cabin and dozed off.

Jane's peaceful sleep was interrupted by Ginny prodding her. "Locks comin' up. Aunty say would yew go an' lockwheel them." Jane scratched her scalp, picked up her windlass and dropped off at the next bridge hole. Striding out, she overtook Billy and checked if there was anything special about these locks. "Naw, just get 'em ready. From now on we's going down all the wiy to Hoxford."

Arriving at the locks Jane found a busy workshop on the bank, with lengthsmen working on lock gates and various bits of equipment. The lock was ready so she fell to chatting with the workmen while she waited for *Fidelity* and found them a friendly bunch. "You'll find the next stretch a bit short of water so take it easy" was their main advice. The five locks took the best part of an hour to work down. At the bottom Nellie remarked "Another seven to Banbury. If they're good we moit make it tonight. Go an' stir that lazy girl off the elum; it's toim she did some work." 'How many ten-year-olds,' wondered Jane, 'would be called lazy just because they were doing a job of work they could sit down to?'

But being sent back to Billy didn't seem to bother young Ginny at all. Clearly her aunt's word was law. Through the late afternoon and into the evening they passed Cropredy and kept going, finally making Banbury as the light was starting to fail. They tied up close by the *Struggler*, another canal people's simple pub with sawdust on the floor. Sometime during the day Nellie had found time to prepare a rabbit stew, and now left Jane cooking the vegetables while Billy was stabled. It had been a gentle day but a long one and Jane dozed off in the pub with the buzz of canal people's voices around her.

The next day was similar: off soon after dawn, intermittent locks through the day and an introduction for Jane to the lifting bridges which crossed the canal at frequent intervals. Simple wooden bridges with hefty balance beams, "Just pull on the beam to lift it then sit on the beam ter keep the bridge up woil the boat goes threw" was all the instruction that was necessary as Jane took her turn on the bank. Progress was good until mid afternoon when they came to Pigeon's Lock; it was under repair and closed to them. Nellie's hopes for getting to Oxford that night evaporated but she was philosophical about it. "It's the koind of thing wat can 'appen," was her only comment. Jane saw it as a good opportunity to see what a lock looked like when drained empty. As well as repair work to a gate and to a ground paddle, two men were raking up rubbish from the bottom of the lock. Among the stuff were four windlasses, including an ornate one with a hardwood handle, a brass cap and finely made metalwork. "Ooh, can I have that?" She asked the lengthsmen.

"Help yerself, dearie" was the laconic answer so she did, taking the ornate one and a spare for the boat. Polished up, the ornate one would make a nice memento of her time on the cut. With nowhere to go, Billy was turned out into an adjacent field, Ginny picked up her crochet and Nellie gave the range a thorough clean and blackleading. With this industry going on round her Jane set to and brought her journal up to date, watched by a curious Ginny. "Yew can read an' write really good?"

"Yes Ginny, I do a lot of it. Can you?"

Ginny shook her head. "I ain't a scholard. Never been in the school. It must be nice ter be able ter do that."

"That really is a shame because it's not difficult to learn. If we had more time I'd try to show you but it would take longer than we have before I've got to go. How long are you staying with your Auntie Nellie?"

Ginny shrugged. "Don't know, maybe 'nother year or two 'till my little sister Mabel can do it. The 'Thority woman says after the war we all must go an' stay in an 'ostel in Brumagen an' go to school. Moi brother Moicle is there now but 'e is special clever so Dad decided to send 'im away. Dad says girls are nothin' special and don' need edyercashun."

"Don't you believe a word of that, Ginny. Girls are just as special and should have just as much education as boys do. That really is a terrible thing to say." Jane found herself getting angry with this casually patriarchal dismissal. "Where is your dad now?"

"Don' know. Last turn was to Brentford but maybe 'e 'as loaded and gone by now."

"So there's no way I could speak to him?"

"Don' do that, please miss. 'E'd be terrible angry with me if yew said anything to 'im."

"Does he hit you?"

Ginny considered this. "Not much. 'E takes his belt to the boys but Mum deals with us girls an' sometimes she wallops us. It's nice bein' 'ere 'cos Auntie Nellie doesn't get cross an' trusts me to do a job fer 'er."

"How many brothers and sister have you got?"

"Six brothers an' five sisters. Mostly they's gone an' there's only Mabel and little Davey left on the boat. The boys 'as been called up an' the girls is mostly married on other boats now. But me an' my sister Angie is both runnerboats fer Aunties wat don' 'ave kids of their own. Oi loiks bein' Auntie's runnerboat."

The aunt passed by at this moment and smiled gently. "You's a good runnerboat too, little Ginny. Oi loiks 'avin' yew 'ere."

Jane smiled. "After this war is over I'm going to try to find you, Ginny, and see if we can't help you get an education. But how long is it going to go on for? I wish I knew."

Again, Ginny shrugged. "Don' think Dad would loik me to go off the cut but we'll see." This casually fatalistic approach to life the canal people all seemed to have was deeply embedded in them and Jane could see it would take more than a passing person off the bank to change it. But it allowed them to be content with their restricted lives on the cut and not hanker too much for anything else. Whether 'anything else' would be any better was debatable too, reflected Jane. They were a healthy, sturdy self-sufficient lot with a strong sense of purpose in their lives and many lifetimes of living so had inured them to the aspects which would be a serious hardship to people accustomed to more salubrious living conditions.

Dawn came soon enough and Jane tumbled out, still heavy with sleep. The lock repair gang turned up about seven o'clock to finish off and tidy their work then the lock was filled. Another horse boat was waiting to lock up so it was taken first, then it was *Fidelity's* turn. But they had a problem: Billy had retired to the farthest corner of his field and showed no desire to get back in harness. Calling him got no response and when Nellie went to get him he moved away just quickly enough not be caught. Cross, she came back to the gate. "Ginny, get the nostern. That'll bring 'im in." But Billy was wise to that one and ignored it until some oats were put in it. Then the crafty old beast ambled over to them trying to look innocent and accepted having his harness put on while he munched. After that they bowhauled the boat into the lock while Billy kept a professional eye on them. But once hitched up he lent his weight against the collar and got going without fuss, leaving Jane with a suspicion that the mule was the really professional one in this team. To begin with the canal was a series of extreme sharp bends and briefly the canal amalgamated with the River Cherwell with sinuous corners and awkward cross-currents, but Billy plodded on and with Nellie on the elum the boat passed safely through this section. A couple more locks and they came to urban Oxford. An inconspicuous little cut led off and Nellie steered the boat into it, coming to a halt at a lock with double gates on it. Waiting at this lock was a man in boater's moleskin trousers, with a large horse. Nellie smiled and waved to this man then explained to Jane: "We're in the Dooks Cut now agen the river an' we'll need extra 'elp. This is 'Enery's cousin Tom 'and 'e will be coming with us to Lechlade to help pull the boat up against the current. Goin' to Lechlade is a special business that we're made for. 'E will sleep in the forecabin an' his hanimal will hitch on ahead of Billy to pull us. It'll be harder work from now on." There was virtually no difference in level either side of the lock so passing through it was quick and easy. As well as his horse, Tom had brought several long shafts which he laid out in the bow of the boat. Introductions made and horse hitched on, they worked the boat down the narrow cut and round sharp bends to see the river Thames ahead of them. As they went Tom briefed Nellie "The river's quiet just now but a bit low. Last stretch into the town we'll be mighty close to the bottom an' we may have to drag the boat a bit." He turned to Jane "You're the Navy girl? I 'ope you're strong. Gettin' through the bridges won't be too bad but we'll still need all your strength."

As the boat pushed into the river the current caught it and swung it out into mid-stream. Jane, on the elum, recognised the movement and swung sharply to counter it as both animals dug in to take the strain. Tom turned to Jane again, "Done this before, then?"

Jane laughed. "Just a bit. I've been working power boats on the tidal lower Thames and we get taken by currents like that all the time."

Tom nodded judiciously. "That'll be handy as we work up. It's easy to get caught out."

"I'll watch for that."

With the two animals pulling and Ginny at their head, progress was good and the first Thames lock came into view. After the narrow locks of the canal, this looked huge. Twice as wide and longer, with wheels to work the paddles, Jane found herself learning again. This time, however, there was an active lock keeper who greeted Tom and Nellie as old friends and worked the lock with them. Meantime the animals were unhitched and led off to the far side of the old stone bridge now in front of them. "Right, Jane, this where we see how strong you are. Come with me." And she was led up to the bow, handed a long pole and told to stand on the right hand side. "Do you know how to quant?"

"Well yes; it will be interesting to see how different this is."

"Fine, try to keep in time with me." And as they emerged from the lock he put his shaft onto the riverbed and pushed. The short distance to the stone bridge gave Jane time to get into the rhythm, but as they shaped up to go through the middle arch their rate of progress dropped, the bridge acting as a natural weir and sharpening the current. "Push hard" she was commanded and slowly they worked the boat through the arch. Ginny was waiting on the far side with the tow rope which she threw expertly at Jane. Grabbing this but not knowing what to do with it she handed it to Tom who hitched it to the tow line from the boat's mast. The animals walked away with the line, lent hard on their collars to take the strain and once more the boat was being pulled from the bank. "That was a bit of a performance, wasn't it?"

"Maybe but the bridges were built without much thought to how you got horse boats through them an' this is how we do it."

"Now I see why Nellie wanted you along as well. Do we have a lot of those?"

"Four plus smaller wooden foot bridges. You'll find a lot of things different on the river."

The first difference was how twisty the river was. Although wider than a canal the river was serpentine in its course, sharp bend following sharp bend in a continuous procession which kept the steerer very alert. In the midst of these the next lock came into view, similar to all the locks on the Upper Thames. The rise was modest: three feet and the upper gates opened. Eventually the sharp bends eased and for some time the boat plodded on until they came round yet another sharp bend to see a pub on the north bank and a flat boat, virtually a raft with low sides, sitting on a slipway on the south bank. Tom smiled, "Right, this will show you something different. Here the towpath changes sides an' the animals have to go across on the ferry. This'll take an hour; do you want to go with 'em and see what happens?"

"Certainly, why not?" With *Fidelity* stemmed on the bank Jane stepped over onto the ferry as Ginny led the horses on. They were evidently used to this as they came without fuss and stood patiently in the middle of the boat. The boat was pushed off for the short crossing but half way over something disturbed Tom's big horse and Ginny went to its head to calm it. It shied and shook its head sending Ginny flying and with a squeak she went over the side. The girl clearly could not swim, thrashing about in the water and shrieking for help. Jane looked at Tom who looked back, shrugged and said, "I can't swim."

"Lot of use you are," Snarled Jane. She whipped her shoes off and dived in. A dozen powerful strokes took her to where Ginny had been but as Jane closed in the girl went under for the second time. Jane duck-dived and fortunately the water was clear enough to see Ginny still flapping feebly. Jane grabbed her, shot to the surface and rolled her onto her back. The current was slight so Jane kicked for the far shore, found a bit of easy access bank and dragged the unconscious body ashore. She picked her up and ran to the pub, now a few hundred yards away and found a firm surface. There she laid Ginny out and applied artificial respiration, pushing then pulling to get water streaming out of her nose and mouth. Ginny coughed violently then started to breathe again; she had survived but it had been a close-run thing. Gently Jane sat her up, rubbing her back and murmuring encouragement. Ginny opened her eyes with terror still in them. "Am I all right?"

"You will be in a few minutes. Just take it easy."

Meanwhile the men had led the horses off the ferry and were waiting. "Will she live?"

"Yes I think so," Said Jane "But she needs a little while to recover. Can we stop here?" By now it was late afternoon; Tom shook his head sadly. "We could do to be gettin' ahead but she comes first. We'll pull the boat over an' tie up for the night. But we'll need to be off at first light tomorrow."

"Oh, all going well she should be fine by then."

The wretched girl was sitting up and shivering violently. "What happened? That 'orrid 'orse knocked me over."

"He knocked you into the river but I don't think he intended to. Something spooked him and he just shook you off. You could do to learn to swim."

Ginny shook her head. "Us boaters don' swim. In a lot of the cut yew can stand on the bottom an' if yew can't yew just drowns. There's allus someone takin' a look in the cut." Again Jane was struck by this fatalistic streak the boat people had. It seemed strange that these people who lived on the water shouldn't swim, but that was their way. A change into dry clothing and a cup of tea went far to restore Ginny but the fright remained at the back of her eyes.

CHAPTER TEN:
Farewell

With the boat bowhauled across the river Nellie bustled round and produced bacon and sausage for the evening meal. Little Ginny, still traumatised, cuddled up to Jane after supper and said "Yew can look after me, can't yew?"

For most of the time Ginny had seemed and behaved like a small adult, but now she was a scared and vulnerable child. Jane, unaccustomed to dealing with children, was at a bit of a loss and could only give her a hug, murmuring "Yes as long as I'm here but you do know I'll be leaving when we get to Lechlade?"

The girl nodded "Yes but yew's 'ere now an' that's good. Oi don' feel so frit wen you's here."

"But surely your Auntie Nellie looks after you?"

"Yes but she don' swim neither so it's nice wen you is here. Is yew a real proper swimmer?"

"Oh yes, I swam for my school in races and did a lot of lifesaving stuff as well."

Ginny nodded wisely and lapsed into silence, comforted by the cuddle.

Nellie and Tom had watched this little scene with gentle amusement. "You've made a hit there, our Ginny's usually fiercely independent."

"Yes well, nearly drowning is enough to shake anyone's confidence and I just happened to be the one who rescued her."

Tom, sitting in the hatchway, asked "What do you think of narrow boat life?"

"I've been fascinated by it. You are all so tough yet loving and caring in your families and there's something rather splendid about the tight bonds that bind you all together. I am very impressed and am going to say so in my report."

Something in this reply was wrong and Tom glared at her. "I s'ppose you're going to describe us as splendid savages, are you? Noble primitives surviving in a world that has moved on round us? D'you think we would live like this if we could get some better way? If you're writing a report, don't patronise us and say what special specimens we are. We's just working people doin' a job that we're skilled at. So don't go back to your office and say what splendid people we are to thrive and strove when you know we'd all be living in a different way if we could."

Jane was startled and taken flat aback by this outpouring, struggling to find anything to say in reply that wouldn't just make it worse. "But Tom, but Tom............. How can I make an honest report that doesn't say some of these things? That's the way you are, as far as I can see, and I've not tried to put myself above you, have I?"

"No, but that educated brain of yours sees us through a filter that can't help condescending to us."

"Oh come on, that's just not true. When have I suggested that I see you as some sort of inferior people, noble savages as you say? I have far more respect for you than that."

"Maybe but all that education you've got in there makes you different from us. We haven't been able to get educated so a lot of us can't even read or write an' someone like you is bound to see us as beneath you."

"Ah, so it's the education thing that bothers you. Well, I can't do much about that except try to understand what it is that makes you so special. Would you be better boat people if you were educated? Or are you better like Ginny here who knows more about the cut and the boats and horses than I'll learn if I stayed here for a year?"

Ginny had been sitting quietly tucked up under Jane's right arm and suddenly spoke. "I'd love ter get edercated an' be able to read 'n write. We's all just workin' like our Billy, doin' wat we knows fer tuppence ha'penny. If we was edercated we'd be able to get jobs on the bank if we wanted an' even if we wanted ter stay on the cut we'd be better at it, an' get paid more. I knows wat I'd like."

This little speech seemed to shut Tom up, and Jane gave the girl a little squeeze of encouragement. For the first time, Nellie spoke. "Y'know, Tom, oi don' find that attertude with Jane. She's adapted ter our way o' livin' without any complaint an' has been really useful wile she's been with us. You's bein' a bit unkind."

"You think so? I've been watching since I joined an' all the time she's thinkin' wat a terrible life we 'ave. I can see it in her face."

"Tom, you allus was a socialist an' now you's seeing things that aren't there. Oi think we'll get a fair deal from Jane an' we should be glad she's come."

"Yes but that's the trouble. Why should we be relying on some outsider ter say nice things 'bout us? We can run our own lives perfectly well without outside interference from some fancypants like Jane."

Jane was getting irritated. "Tom, this fancypants is only here to see if girls off the bank could work on the boats. You know there's a big shortage of crew and blokes aren't available because they're all called up. That's not interference and I suspect you know it. It's you who is seeing the world through a filter of your own resentments about lack of education. Well, you just heard what Ginny had to say and that's what the future holds, so get used to it and be glad of it."

Ginny stirred. "Oi'm goin' ter bed. Yous can go to the pub if you wants to go on arguin'."

Tom went but Nellie and Jane elected to stay on the boat and get an early night.

With Tom gone, Nellie said "Don't mind him, Jane. He's allus loik that an' would argue with the Devil himself."

Jane smiled gently. "Trouble is, Nellie, there's a half-truth behind what he's saying. You people must get no end of do-gooders and officials poking their noses into your way of life and some of them are bound to adopt a top-lofty sort of tone. I'll bet that infuriates you sometimes."

"Sometimes yes, but that's just wat 'appens to us an' we 'as to live with it. You's been different 'cos you 'as got stuck in and strove. Oi reckon that means we'll get a good report from you."

Above all, what was bearing in on Jane's thinking was that there could be a lot resting on her report. It might just get ignored, of course, but if it was taken at all seriously it might make a difference to these decent people. As she blew up her mattress and settled for the night this thought went round and round in her mind.

Getting up at first light was becoming natural but even so Jane found she was the last one up. Tom was on the bank with the animals, Nellie was stoking the stove and little Ginny came wandering back from the pub with, "It is nice ter get a wash." There was a friendly, "Mornin' Jane," from Tom as though last night's debate had never happened and in no time they were on the move again. They had to wait half an hour for the lock-keeper to emerge at the first lock but that gave them time for breakfast: a fried egg in a sandwich with lots of tea. For some time the river was straighter and trundling along at horse plus mule speed they made good time. This part of the river had a remote beauty to it, virtually no sign of human habitation or activity and it was hard to grasp that they were passing through one of the more occupied areas of England. Seriously sharp bends came up at intervals as did more bridges which they had to quant their way through, but the river being low the current was not strong and getting through the bridges did not impede them seriously. "You should try these wen the river's in spate," remarked Tom when Jane commented that the bridges were not as much of an obstacle as she had expected. The river got seriously wiggly again and Jane on the elum found herself working hard to keep the boat going round corner after corner. Into the afternoon they pushed on with locks and bridges coming up every now and then. Nellie, taking over the elum remarked, "We should get ter Lechlade tonight. We's makin' real good progress." Some more wiggles, St John's lock and a last stone bridge and Lechlade was in front of them. A final twenty minutes took them to the coal wharf where they tied up in the early evening. Animals stabled and given a good rub down, there was a general sense of relaxing, destination in hand. Jane bought fish and chips for everyone as a parting gesture. Ginny, despite her skinny little frame, disposed of a full adult portion plus some chips sneaked from Nellie's.

After the previous night's debate there was little appetite for talking; Tom took himself off to the pub, Ginny took herself off to bed and Nellie settled to her crochet so Jane brought her journal up to date and started packing.

She was awake at first light but there was nothing to do so she rolled over and tried to sleep again. But getting up at this hour was so ingrained by now that she just lay there wide awake, finally giving up and getting dressed by six a/m. After breakfast she helped take down the side cloths then it was time for Jane to go. There was a tearful farewell and a sudden passionate hug from Ginny, warm thanks exchanged with Nellie and a brief handshake with Tom then, kitbag on shoulder, she was on her way to the station. The local stopping train hauled by a neat little pannier tank engine took her slowly to Oxford where she treated herself to a first-class ticket to Paddington. Totally unaware of how filthy and scruffy she was, she got some very funny looks and the odd harrumph from the other denizens in the compartment she chose, but lost in a reverie of locks and mules she ignored them. Jane had written to Lady Ormond warning of her imminent arrival which meant that when she presented herself at the door the butler was expecting her. Even so, his eyes widened with surprise when he saw Jane's condition. Lady O was equally taken aback. "Jane! What on earth have you been doing? I thought you were on a canal, not down a coal mine."

"Well there's not much in the way of facilities on these narrow boats and they do a lot of fairly dirty work. Add dirty bits of canal to that and it's a miracle they aren't all like me. It's all healthy open air stuff but the filth at times can be overwhelming. I do hope I can have a decent bath now."

"Yes of course Jane and I will arrange for my hairdresser to come later today and sort your haystack out. Do you need a manicurist?"

Jane snorted with amusement, looking at the battered claws her hands had become, with ingrained grime, broken nails, assorted cuts and bruises and calluses harder and shinier than any she had ever had. "I can't help thinking a manicurist would just give up in despair, so let's scrub round that one."

CHAPTER ELEVEN:
Re-Entry

The bath was pure luxury. She had a first soak just to get the dirt scrubbed off then defied regulations by running a second bath, sinking into it and just luxuriating in its warmth and enveloping comfort. She emerged feeling a great deal better, pulled on a dressing gown and started to open the substantial pile of mail that was waiting for her. Three letters from fiancé David got first attention. He had been in the shipyard standing by his ship as it was re-constructed, new boilers and condenser installed, main engines stripped and overhauled, and the new bow building up nicely. At the end of each letter a couple of paragraphs of personal feelings were added but rather disappointingly seemed a routine add-on lacking any deeper emotion, rather than anything intimate to a fiancé.

The arrival of the hairdresser pulled Jane away from her correspondence. This lady's first reaction to the state of her hair was to cluck and shake her head in disbelief, but on hearing the story of Jane falling head first into the mud, she realised she had a challenge on her hands. An hour of cleaning, trimming and shaping had the mullet looking presentable again and complying with Wren regulations. Some mousse rubbed into it brought the shine back, white streak prominent; Jane had never been particularly vain about her hair but somehow getting it to look good again restored a different, more personal, sort of confidence in herself than Jane had felt for the last few weeks. Then it was back to the letters. David would be getting away from his ship for a long weekend. The thought of this togetherness with him stirred a warmth and longing she hadn't noticed during her intensely focussed time on the narrow boats and was something to look forward to. The other important letter was from Third Officer Baker at headquarters so was official. It instructed that on leaving the canals Jane was to telephone right away and be ready to come into Wren headquarters to write her report. A week was being allocated for her to complete it. Jane considered this: with her copious journal to hand and an outline formed in her mind already, that should not be difficult. The letter then continued: ten day's leave was due to her; Jane's thought was that that would allow her time to visit her family, but in turn that would depend on what David was doing. Certainly it was high time she visited her neglected family again. The rest of the letter then re-confirmed that after leave she was booked onto a one-month signals course from tenth August; her impending wedding was noted and at present there should not be any problem in her having time off for that. From early October she would be assigned to the staff group preparing for the first boat crew Wrens' course at Plymouth.

Jane was pulled out of her letters by Edith the maid announcing dinner.

Although Lady Ormond's establishment was relatively informal Lady O always changed for dinner so Jane decided to do the same and put on one of her long white evening gowns. Its silky softness was a slinky contrast to the battered remnants of uniform that she had worn in the last few weeks and went some way to restoring a sense of being feminine. Seated, Lady Ormond said "Now Jane, tell me all about our canals. I understand they are still commercially active?"

Well yes, said Jane and she launched off into a tale of motor pairs and mule drawn horseboats, of locks and of bowhauling on the Bottom Road; this went on for some time.

"Do I understand that you have acquired a strong respect for these nomads?"

"O God yes, they are wonderful people, a bit rough perhaps but such genuine workers with this intense sense of family unity and pride in their craft. There's a lesson there for all of us."

"How interesting. They really have touched you deeply. I suppose all this work has left you even fitter and stronger?"

"Fitter and stronger? I could take on Samson just now and throw him over my shoulder. Working the canals is enough to harden every muscle in your body. But really that's a side-effect of the way of life with its constant pressure to get ahead and of the very basic physicality of how everything works. If you are fully involved in the work and lifestyle of the canal people you can't help but end up fit and strong, not that I was feeble before; but that life in the open air and in the countryside is so healthy. As you'll gather, I just loved it. Now, I haven't heard a news for a month. How is the war going?"

"Well I suppose the main event is that Germany has invaded Russia. They went in on the twenty-second of June and so far appear to be storming through to Moscow. But my contacts tell me that in the end Russia will just absorb the Boches then throw them out again. If Napoleon couldn't do it, neither will Hitler and it just might be the mistake that costs him the war. Needless to say our military are delighted with the way it takes the pressure off Britain and all of a sudden the Soviet Union has become our best friend."

"Good Heavens. If Hitler succeeds he will be able to link up with Japan and that might be very bad news for us. How about the Navy?"

"We are still being beaten by the U-boats and are losing far too many ships in the Atlantic but apart from that the Mediterranean seems to be the main area for action. There's a lot of pushing and pulling although we are managing to keep Malta going. There's more fighting going on in North Africa where this General Rommel has transformed the effectiveness of the Axis armies. Since the British army was chucked out of Crete we seem to have been on the back foot just about everywhere. Not good but we keep on plodding away as best we can."

"Yes, that seems to be what we are best at."

By now coffee and a quite acceptable port were being served, and Jane couldn't help but have an ironic smile at the contrast; on the boat it would have been yet another cup of tea and whatever was available to make a sweet sandwich.

Sinking into a soft double bed was strange after the weeks of lying on her narrow airbed. She lay awake thinking over the experiences of the last few weeks. It had all been so utterly different to anything else she had known that it was difficult to put it in context. Out there the boat people were getting ahead, working dawn to dusk doing heavy physical labour and taking as normal, cold wet living conditions with just the strength of their family connections as a central stability. Little Ginny, just ten years old, was working full days of demanding adult-level physical effort and treating that as the natural order of things. Here Jane was lying in soft luxury which almost seemed offensive and out of proportion contrasted with the harshness she had lived with these past few weeks.

Unbidden, a line from a folk song the choir had sung at school came into her mind: *'And she went with the raggle-taggle gypsies O'*. At the time running away from home comforts had seemed like a very silly idea to Jane's practical nature. Now, it sort of made sense. *'O why do you leave your house and your land?'* exclaims her Lord when he finds His Lady in a field with a gypsy, to which her reply had been *'What do I care for my house and my land?'* and *'What do I care for my goose feather bed?'* Jane rolled over uneasily in the feathered softness she now lay in. *'Tonight I'll lie in a wide open field, in the arms of my gypsy-O.'* No wonder her lord had been a bit upset, but now Jane could see some reason for the lady's behaviour. Allowing for the boat people being very annoyed if they were classed with gypsies, the similarities were striking. The way she felt now, Jane would have no difficulty lying in a field or a narrow boat's sidebed instead of her present voluptuous comfort and it was an appealing thought. The life of the boat people with its direct, harsh but true way of life seemed very tempting. Was her regimented and conformist life in uniform a way of avoiding taking responsibility for herself? She had never thought so but then she had never encountered a group like the boat people, so disciplined in performing their work but with a discipline entirely of their own making. The deep loving bonds the families had for each other had been a revelation too. In their closed–off restless world, family was all the solidity they had and its powerful links kept the social fabric of the boater community together through every challenge.

And what of David? Her fiancé and great love had an unreality as did his home at Hemel Towers and people like the Marchioness. In its own way that gilded life-style from another world was as isolated from everyday society as the boat peoples' had been. She was committed to this fiancé of hers and to becoming his Naval wife which would probably produce a restricted and tightly regimented lifestyle; suddenly she had grave doubts about whether she wanted to live that way. Perhaps she might run away and join the boat people, live in their raw but true world like the raggle-taggle gypsy's lady? No, that was silly really but the temptation was there and the inevitable stifling conformity of life at Hemel Towers and as an officer's wife, a daunting thought. She could just imagine what her own Lord would have to say about her present doubts and hankerings. 'Oh David,' she thought 'I only hope the magic rekindles when we meet.' She lay awake for some time struggling with these thoughts. Turning the notion over in her mind, she thought of the boat people's social structure and asked herself, 'would I really want to live in a world as backward as theirs? Where the men rule and the women do the work? It's bad enough dealing with the Navy without deliberately putting myself under the thumb of some bloke who would regard that as the normal order of things and expect to lord it over me. At least as a Wren I have a little bit of autonomy and my own place. On the cut I'd just be one more female worker. No, on balance going back to them is not a good idea but their particular sort of freedom is such a temptation.' All these jumbling thoughts made for a poor night's sleep.

Waking at dawn and being ready to start the day when the rest of the household were still sound asleep was rather more of an inconvenience. By the time Edith the maid appeared with early morning tea Jane had been up and dressed for some time, and was engrossed in her correspondence again. Preparing for the day, she did not enjoy getting back into uniform with its white shirt and starched detached collar. After breakfast a quick phone call to Merle confirmed that she was to come in right away to be set up with entry pass and arrangements for getting her report typed up. By late morning Jane was presenting herself to a cautious sentry at the entrance. She was escorted to the Wrens HQ and handed over to Third Officer Baker who greeted Jane in friendly fashion. "Hello Jane, back to the real world, eh?"

"Hello Merle. It's debatable which is the real world but here I am, ready to report."

"That's good. The director wants to see you at 1600 for a short debrief. In the meantime I'll get your pass organised and make arrangements for your report. Can you type?"

"Afraid not, Merle, but my handwriting is reasonably clear so if my handwritten draft can be given to a typist she should be able to type it up without too much difficulty."

"That should be fine. Would you like a coffee?"

"Ooh yes please, last night was the first one of those I'd had for a month. Lashings of tea on the boats but no coffee."

Jane quickly settled to writing her report, and by 1600 had started to get it into order. Summoned into the presence, she had to remember her drill and report in correct fashion. The director looked at her coolly. "Right Beacon, give me a fifteen minute summary. I gather you had more variety of experience than we had originally planned for."

"Yes ma'am, in a way the motor boat breaking down was a blessing in disguise as it meant I got a much wider view of work on the canals than I would otherwise have. Working on a single horse-drawn boat is very different from a motor pair."

"What conclusions have you come to about Wrens on the boats?"

"A bit of a mixture, ma'am. The canal people are a very close-knit community based on families with their own language and ways of doing things. It is still a very patriarchal society where women are expected to do what they are told although they do have their own ways of getting back at their men." This got a wry smile of recognition from the Director. "One way and another I have serious doubts about whether adding a strange Wren into any of these family groups would work. There is no reason why reasonably strong and fit women should not be able to work on the narrow boats, but I feel that they would be more effective making up whole crews of their own. But that said it seems to me that a militarised structure, even just for administrative purposes, would be inappropriate. These people are the most untamed and independent that I've ever encountered and the whole system is set up for them to run their boats as they chose, get their cargo orders then go their own way to deliver it. Because they only get paid by the cargoes they carry, there is an economic imperative on them all the time which produces its own version of discipline without anything being imposed from outside. They are wonderfully friendly and hospitable people but only on their own terms and I just don't see the WRNS adding anything to that. If you like, let women be recruited directly onto the narrow boats rather than having the Wrens structure in the way."

Jane paused to think over what else to say. "Another consideration is that they have their own social structures with a very strict moral code: it is a fallacy that they are loose living. They marry among their own kind and I suspect that introducing stray young women from outside into this structure might be very disruptive no matter how well behaved our girls might intend to be. Not an easy position for an odd Wren to live with. Also it is steerers – that is captains – of the boats that they are short of, now that so many have been called up into the services. It would take a lot of training to get girls able to do that and even then the boating families would never accept anyone from outside being put over them so again it would have to be crews made up entirely of girls off the bank."

"I see. This is very interesting stuff and you are to be congratulated on coming to such clear conclusions even if they are not what I had hoped for. When you write your report, put these conclusions in a summary on the front page so that they are immediately accessible."

"Very good ma'am."

"How long will it take you to produce this report?"

"I kept up a journal throughout and that gives me all the raw material I need. Third Officer Baker tells me I have a week to get it done and with adequate typing support there's no reason why I shouldn't get it done in that time. Will that be satisfactory?"

"I should think so, Beacon. I would appreciate it if you left your journal with us as well so we can get a copy of that typed up. Can I take it that there are no intimate secrets in it?"

Jane laughed. "None at all ma'am. I might perhaps like to get it back eventually as a souvenir but no rush about it."

"All right then, Beacon. Have you anything else to raise with me?"

"Only the personal matter that I am getting married in September. Third Officer Baker thinks that I can get time off for that before going to Plymouth in early October to join the staff for the boat crew Wrens' training course."

"I see. Does this mean you will be leaving the Wrens? We had rather counted on your being available for some time yet."

"No Ma'am it does not. My fiancé is Lieutenant-Commander Lord David Daubeny-Fowkes and he will be going back to sea once his ship is repaired. As long as we can manage to co-ordinate our leaves there is no reason why I shouldn't stay in the Wrens for the duration."

"No babies then?"

Jane smiled. "No planned ones, that's for sure, and I know enough to avoid most accidents. Starting a family will have to wait for demob unless this horrid war goes on for a very long time. But I am only twenty-one so I can afford to wait a few years before settling for domestic bliss."

"I know of the Daubeny-Fowkes as a political family. Is your fiancé a professional Navy man?"

"Yes indeed ma'am. He's the youngest of his family and free to make his own way within the constraints of wanting a full career as a Naval officer."

"I shall rely on Third Officer Baker to keep me informed of your circumstances but I do hope you will continue to serve. For now go to it and write your report."

"Aye aye ma'am."

Jane saluted and marched off in proper fashion, mind on the report and how she would write it. After her month of freedom she was transitioning back into being a Wren, under discipline and orders. Settling into that again might not be as easy as once it was. Even if she was no longer on it, the call of the cut was still strong and the independent self-reliance she had learned would stay with her.

* * *

WOMENS' ROYAL NAVAL SERVICE
REPORT ON INVESTIGATION INTO THE FEASIBILITY OF WRENS PROVIDING CREWS FOR NARROW BOATS.
BY
Petty Officer Wren Jane Beacon

SUMMARY OF CONCLUSIONS

In June/July 1941 I was tasked with making a trip on a narrow boat to investigate whether WRNS personnel might make up crews for these freight carrying canal craft.

I made a trip on a motor pair from Limehouse Basin by way of the Grand Union Canal to Tyseley, Birmingham then to the Coventry coal fields to load coal for London. At Hawkesbury Junction the motor boat suffered a breakdown and I transferred to the horseboat 'Fidelity', on which I travelled via the Oxford Canal and Upper Thames to Lechlade where I left the boat. My conclusions in answer to the question posed are as follows:

1.   The narrow boats are crewed by families and the whole social structure of the canal operating system is a tightly knit web of family units. These people live in their own world with little contact with the wider world and in consequence have evolved their own standards and way of life. Most of these families have been on the canal boats for generations.
2.   It would be very difficult for outsiders to enter this world and be accepted by the families on the boats. While the families are very hospitable to visiting 'outsiders' It appeared to me that they would be much less accepting of having individuals from outside placed with them on a long-term, working, basis.
3.   The work is gruelling and non-stop. There is a heavy physical demand on the crews, working their way through the multitude of locks on the canal system, all of which are operated by hand. The crews commonly work from dawn to dusk which means up to a fourteen hour day every day. The family members are accustomed to this from childhood but it is very wearing for anyone not used to it.

4.   The whole way of working and living, now delivering cargoes of much needed war materials has evolved over time to be highly efficient. The boats with their operating families are paid by the cargo delivered which creates its own discipline in the need to 'get ahead' and earn their freights. Within the boats the traditional family structure with a man as head of the unit, his wife and however many children, form a working team with a version of the discipline to be found in any family, but bent to a particular purpose. It is difficult to see how the militarised structure of the WRNS has anything to add to this very different but very effective way of living and working.

5.   There is no reason why fit and strong women should not work canal boats. The life is outdoor and healthy and if such women can adjust to the very basic living conditions they could make up whole crews for narrow boats perfectly well, given training. The canal families make the work look easy but this is deceptive, with skills based on a life-time's experience and new-comers to the canals would need time to learn and adjust to the way of life. But as with point four, this does not justify any overarching control from the WRNS.

Glossary

Agen corruption of against. A broad term meaning next to, alongside, beside, close to etc.

Animal Or as the boat people called them 'Hanimal'. A horse/pony/mule/donkey used to pull an unpowered boat along.

The Bank General term for the land. Off the bank was anyone or anything coming onto the canals (the 'cut') from the land. Going on the bank meant leaving the canals for the land.

Barge Any wide-beamed canal craft, usually of 14 feet beam or more.

Boat Any narrow boat with a beam of 7feet to fit the canal system's narrow locks.

Bottom Road The Birmingham and Fazeley Canal, curving north-east from Birmingham then south east.

Bow Hauling Pulling boats by hand, usually into or out of a lock. Hard and heavy work.

Breasting up Tying both boats of a pair alongside each other.

Butty The unpowered second boat of a narrow boat pair.

Going Butty When two narrow boat pairs work together through locks and along difficult sections of canal.

Crosher Corruption of crochet, a favourite artistic habit of the canal women.

The Cut Universally used term for the canals.

Drawing Lifting the paddles of a lock.

Gauging using a special measuring stick to find how deep in the water a boat is. This defines how much cargo is on board and hence what canal dues have to be paid.

Good Road	When the locks are set available for a boat to enter on arrival. Conversely a 'bad road' is when the locks are against the approaching boats and have to be filled or emptied before they can enter the lock.
Elum	Corruption of 'Helm'. The steering arrangement and area from which boats are steered. More narrowly, the tiller used to work the rudder. The Ram's Head is the highly decorated top of the rudder post of a butty or horse boat.
Lock Wheeling	Having a member of a boat's crew go ahead (often on a bicycle) to set a lock ready for the boat's arrival.
Wheeler	The person sent ahead is the 'wheeler'.
Mangle	Two roller wringer for washed, still wet, clothes
Moty	Horseboat people's term for motor powered narrow boats
Nostern	The metal can nosebag for feeding the horse on the move.
Number Ones	Owners of their own boats.
Pound	A length of canal without locks
Quant (ing)	A term widely used in boat communities of all sorts. Pushing a boat along by dropping a pole onto the bed of a watercourse and pushing on it. Punting is a version of the same activity.
Runnerboat	Corruption of runabout. A child (usually but not necessarily a girl) lent by one part of a family to another without children of their own, to help run the borrowers' boats.
Shaft	Long poles used to move a boat around.
Snubber	The long tow-rope between motor and butty when 'lengthened out'. Normally seventy feet long.
Stemmed up	Going aground in the canal or jammed in a lock
Straps	General name for ropes used in securing or handling the boats.

Strove	Past tense of 'strive'. General term used by boaters for doing physical work.
Stud	T-shaped cleats for making fast ropes to.
Taking a look	Boaters' term for falling into the canal.
Wind	Rhymes with 'pinned'. To turn a boat around. A winding hole is a widened bit of canal in which boats can turn.
Windlass	The L-shaped iron handle with a squared ring on one end. Fits onto paddle gear at locks for winding them up or down.

A FEW ROYAL NAVAL EXPRESSIONS

Guzz	Plymouth, and in particular the Naval base at Devonport.
Killick	Leading Seaman. Equivalent to corporal in the Army.
Pompey	Portsmouth

BIBLIOGRAPHY

TITLE	AUTHOR	PUBLISHER
HISTORIC		
A Canal People	Sonia Rolt	The History Press
Life on the Canal	Anthony Burton	Pitkin
Voices from the Waterways	Jean Stone	Sutton Publishing Ltd.
Narrow Boat	L T C Rolt	Eyre & Spottiswoode
Landscape with Canals	L T C Rolt	Sutton Publishing Ltd
Ramlin Rose	Sheila Stewart	Oxford University Press
IDLE WOMEN		
Troubled Waters	Margaret Cornish	Robert Hale
Maidens' Trip	Emma Smith	Bloomsbury
The Amateur Boatwomen	Eily Gayford	The Belmont Press
Idle Women	Susan Wolfitt	M & M Baldwin
GENERAL		
No. 1	Tom Foxon	J M Pearson & Son
Tracing your Canal Ancestors	Sue Wilkes	Pen & Sword
GUIDES		
A Canal Companion, Oxford & Grand Union, and Upper Thames		J M Pearson & Sons Ltd
Souvenir Guide to Ellesmere Port Canal Museum National Waterways Trust		
FICTION		
A Boy off the Bank	Geoffrey Lewis	S G M Publishing
A Girl at the Tiller	Geoffrey Lewis	S G M Publishing
FILM		
Painted Boats	Producer Michael Balcon Director Charles Crichton	

Printed in Poland
by Amazon Fulfillment
Poland Sp. z o.o., Wrocław

49685204R00054